OMEGA GRAY

SEB DOUBINSKY

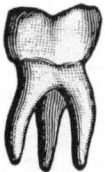

Bizarro Pulp Press
an imprint of JournalStone Publishing

This is a work of fiction. All of the characters, names, incidents, organizations, and dialogue in this novel are either the products of the author's imagination or are used fictitiously.

Bizarro Pulp Press books may be ordered through booksellers or by contacting:

Bizarro Pulp Press, a JournalStone imprint
    www.BizarroPulpPress.com

    ISBN: 978-1-942712-95-4

Printed in the United States of America
JournalStone rev. date: January 16, 2016

    Cover Art: Matthew Revert
        www.matthewrevert.com
    Interior Formatting: Lori Michelle
        www.theauthorsalley.com

TO JAMES GODDARD.

PRAISE FOR SEB DOUBINSKY

"Seb Doubinsky has a rare talent: his imagination outstrips nature."
James Greer, author of *Artificial Light* and *The Failure*

"Doubinsky's style is as stark as a winter tree."
Vanessa Veselka, author of *Zazen*

"In the intense and frightening fiction of Seb Doubinsky, a character is in grave danger if he or she thinks independently or displays any real humanity."
Matt Bialer, author of *Ascent*.

"Doubinsky is astonishingly entertaining."
Michael Moorcock

"So it goes."
Kurt Vonnegut

1. LEAF GREEN.

1. JUNGLE JIM

1.

PROFESSOR TODD BAILER let out a deep sigh and stopped in his tracks to grab the water bottle from his backpack. His spine was sticky with sweat, his forehead on fire and he felt his frizzy, graying hair stoop like rain-gorged moss over his receding hairline. Not to mention the little blood spots left by the dead bugs he had smashed all over his cheeks. Luis, his guide, had told him to wear a hat and a net over his face, but the idea of looking like a 19th century British Lady explorer had made him decline. Now he knew those ladies had been smart.

Luis turned around and tapped his watch, indicating his impatience. Bailer nodded and twisted off the cap of the bottle. The water made him gurgle with delight. At the hotel they'd gotten up at five and had already driven three hours; first on a destroyed asphalt road, then on rough terrain covered with hostile vegetation, until it had become impossible for the Range Rover to go further.

Bailer thought about the Conquistadores making their way across South America on foot. *Must have worn nothing under their heavy armors*. The idea of Spanish mercenaries in rusty plates with their genitals hanging out made him chuckle.

"Señor, we must be going," Luis whined. "We still have a long way to go."

Bailer nodded again, putting the bottle back in its bag. He was glad that this was work, and not a vacation. At least, he was not spending his own money. *"Hell Trek in the Jungle! Experience real dysentery, real mosquitoes and real boredom!"* To say nothing of the blisters he was feeling growing on the soles of his feet. All of this

3

in the name of science . . . He sighed and followed Luis, who had begun macheting his way through the jungle again.

2.

"*Eso es mi amigo*, Professor Bailer," Luis said.

The shaman, a walking skeleton with painted circles all over his skinny body and a few matted feathers jammed through his greasy grey hair, looked at him with piercing black eyes and spat on the ground.

Luis smiled politely and looked away. Bailer extended a hand and the shaman spat again, this time right between his feet.

The smell of the jungle surrounded them, a pungent, watery, overwhelming smell. It was the first time Bailer had ever found himself in such hostile territory—such radically hostile territory. Although he had supported native movements with small donations all his life, he was beginning to see the attraction of comfort.

He recalled, with a pang of retrospective incredulity, his joy when he had learned that his project had been accepted by the academic research board and that the funds had been sent to his research account. He'd thought, "The jungle! The jungle!" Now he knew he should have instead remembered, "The horror! The horror!"

The shaman pointed at him and said something to Luis.

"He-who-has-six-eyes says you're big."

Bailer nodded, not knowing how to answer.

"It's good," Luis added. "It means you have less chances of dying."

Bailer nodded again. *Oh shit,* he thought.

The shaman mumbled something else, this time pointing at a palm-leaf thatched rundown building with no walls at the other end of the small village.

"The ceremony will take place tonight. It'll be 200 dollars."

Bailer's eyebrows lifted in painful surprise. That was basically all the cash he was carrying, give or take a few dollars.

"That's because you're my friend." Luis explained. "Special price."

Luis smiled. The shaman smiled. Bailer forced a smile and

nodded. A song kept playing in his overheated brain—"Running Through The Jungle." He hoped it wasn't an omen.

3.

Why am I doing this? Bailer thought as the toothless shaman, "He-who-has-six-eyes—and-two-teeth" as he had secretly nicknamed him, passed the dirty plastic bowl on to him. It was filled with a disgusting yellow bile-looking liquid with a few banana flies floating on the surface. *At least they died happy,* Bailer chuckled to himself and hesitated as he lifted the stained bowl.

All the men of the village were sitting around him, some already high on the beverage. They were drooling filaments of yellowish saliva, standing up every now and then to go and throw up noiselessly in the bushes behind the large open hut. The women and children, who were forbidden to take part, had stayed in their huts. Night was falling, but it was still very hot and humid. Bailer wiped his forehead with the back of his hand, instinctively shut his eyes and took a sip of the repulsive liquid.

He grimaced, eyes still closed.

It was as disgusting as it looked.

He resisted his envy to spit it out and swallowed most of it, letting the rest seep through his clenched lips and over his trembling chin. He handed the bowl to Luis, who shook his head.

"I need to stay clear-headed, in case something goes wrong," he explained, passing the bowl onto the man sitting next to him.

Bailer nodded and felt the surge of a violent nausea. He stood up in a hurry and followed a man into the bushes. There he heaved continuously for fifteen minutes. He checked his watch every now and then, so he could scientifically describe the experiment later in his report.

When he could finally straighten up again and look around, night had fallen and he was feeling very, very drunk. He painstakingly made his way back to the ceremonial building, still nauseous, his legs feeling as if they were made of lead. Strange lights danced in front of his eyes. *Insects*, he thought. *Fireflies*. Then the insects changed color and the trees flashed a violent pink light, which engulfed him whole.

4.

The nausea had gone, Bailer realized with relief when he opened his eyes. But, to his horror, so had the jungle. Night had disappeared too, replaced by a blinding, cloudless blue sky. He was standing on a long white beach where what looked like two Greek or Roman armies—he was no expert—were about to massacre each other.

What the fuck is going on? Where am I? Where's the jungle?

The warriors, who wore shiny bronze helmets with long red manes, bore long spears and round shields decorated with strange images, were running towards each other, screaming things Bailer interpreted as insults or rallying cries. Their collision was so formidable that he felt the shockwave in the sand under his feet. Helmets fell on the sand, bits of armor flew up in the air, weapons clashed with sparks. It was as beautiful as it was terrifying. As the fighting armies drifted towards him, full of noise and violence, Bailer felt completely helpless and turned around to flee for safety.

That's when he bumped into private eye Joe M.

5.

"You all right, pal?" the PI asked, putting his hand on Bailer's shoulder. "You look badly shaken up."

Joe M.

His favorite TV show as a kid. It was an old 70s series, but he loved the colors, the clothes, the noir plots. The actor's name was Mitch Conrad. It was the first show that had featured a Black woman as a recurrent character, his secretary, Daisy.

LSD 25. LSD 25. LSD 25. This is a hallucination. I've never taken LSD 25 in my life, but I'm sure this is the way it works. I've read all the books and articles. Random mental associations. I'm freaking out. Seen the movies too. It's only a bad trip. I'm just freaking out.

Trying to muster a fragment of coherence, Bailer smiled at the apparition.

"Mitch Conrad?"

The man shook his head.

"No, Joe M. Looking for someone called Mitch Conrad?

Obviously, you're not dead. You're a Floater. Intentional? Accidental?"

"What?"

As his eyes got used to the harsh light, Bailer suddenly realized that Joe M. wasn't alone on the beach. A huge crowd was present, looking like the front cover of the Beatles' *Sergeant Pepper Lonely Hearts' Club Band*. They wore all sorts of costumes, as in a demented historical carnival. He also thought he saw Zorro on his horse. Behind them, like a crazy Modernist's dream, a huge city loomed, with skyscrapers, Zeppelins, hot-air balloons and helicopters.

LSD 25. Freak out.

"You're not covered in blood," Joe M. remarked. "Then you must be intentional. Who are you looking for? Maybe I can help you . . . Tell me more about that Mitch Conrad . . . "

Bailer looked at himself. He was wearing the same clothes as he'd worn in the jungle. No blood, no. Definitely no blood.

He was about to ask Joe M. how he could get back to the jungle when night suddenly fell again and everything turned black.

6.

First, there was the smell. Earthy, humid, nauseating. Then the voice.

"*Señor! Señor!* Are you ok? Wake up, *Señor* . . . "

Luis.

Bailer groaned and slowly opened his eyes.

Words in Spanish and another language . . . Mumbo-jumbo . . .

"*Señor!*"

A mole hill obscured his view and his cheek was bathed in something warm and wet. The hill moved. He recognized a shoe.

More Spanish.

Hands grabbed him firmly and lifted him. Colors whirled before his eyes, similar to the patterns you see when you press your closed eyelids with your fingers. Except his eyes were wide open.

As he was turned around to be carried away, he saw the earth become sky, in a whirl of green, brown and grey.

7.

"Amazing, but inconclusive," Bailer said, shaking his head.

He was sitting on a wooden stool in the shaman's hut, still feeling queasy, but otherwise good. He had been comatose all afternoon, attended by a couple of young women who had tried to force strange food and tepid water through his clenched lips. Then, little by little, he felt better and managed to sit up. Luis had been called and he hugged him, as if he had survived some extraordinary accident.

"You're alive!"

"You sound surprised," Bailer grumbled, half-joking.

"I am, señor . . . You reacted very strongly . . . Was it the first time you ingested hallucinogens? Usually, those who come here have an old history . . . But you . . . "

Bailer smiled as proudly as he could.

"I've tried a lot of them," he lied. "I had a wild youth."

As if. Still, he was happy to be alive. Luis had left and he had remained alone in the hut, thinking back on what he had seen. The hoplites, or whatever they were called. The city. Joe M. *Fucking Joe M.!* He laughed out loud. What a trip. He now understood the psychedelic culture better. Kids with no scientific background seeing this . . . Wow. No wonder they said it was mind-expanding . . . But he was a man of science and his brain was telling him: hallucination. Pure and simple.

"Hallucination. Pure and simple. Extremely powerful, but I definitely wasn't in the Kingdom of the Dead. What's more, I didn't see any light at the end of the tunnel . . . "

Luis translated to the Shaman, who spat on the ground between his own legs. He sat across Bailer, fanning himself with a palm leave.

"What light? He asks," Luis translated. "He says he has never seen any light, and he doesn't know what a tunnel is. I actually had to translate it as burrow, which doesn't make much sense either. "

Bailer shrugged.

"Never mind."

The Shaman cackled.

"He wants to know if you've seen the city by the sea, with the high buildings. And the strange people."

Bailer hid his surprise, but nodded anyway.

"Yes, I did. But that doesn't prove anything. The brain functions on archetypes. What he calls a city and what I call a city can be two very different things."

Luis translated and the Shaman stood up and walked to the other end of his large hut. He moved some things and came back with a large piece of dried wood. He handed it to Bailer, looking him straight in the eyes. The scientist took it, feeling uneasy because of the intense scrutiny.

There were crude drawings on the wood, hard to see in the darkness of the hut, but Bailer recognized what they represented. A city, the sea, and various places indicated with abstract glyphs. The Shaman spoke again, but this time his voice was trembling with rage.

"This is a map of the Land of the Dead," Luis translated. "This is where he goes when he wants to talk to his ancestors. Always same place. Always same people."

Bailer smiled as nicely as he could, handing the piece of wood back to the Shaman who snatched it violently from his hands.

Always same place because always same brain, you fool, he thought, but he kept smiling as he slowly stood up.

"Luis, can you thank He-Who-Has-Six-Eyes for me. It's been a fantastic experience. Really."

Luis translated to the Shaman who had remained seated. He nodded, spat on the ground and extended a hand.

"200 dollars," Luis said.

8.

Feeling refreshed by the hot shower, Bailer lay on his bed with his laptop on his thighs. He checked the data he had gathered from the trip in the jungle. Joe M.! He would have to find funds for India, Mongolia, Australia and Africa . . . He hoped the reference to Joe M. wouldn't compromise his chances. For a split second he considered editing it from his report, but his scientific mind protested loudly. He was a scientist and science was truth. The whole truth. What's more, there aren't real failures in experimental science—it is, after all, a question of trial and error, and recognizing a failure is as important as seeing a success. At least, he hoped the university's Research Committee would see it that way . . .

Putting his computer aside, he stood up and walked to the window of the small but clean hotel of Santa Esperanza, looking down at the noisy and colorful street outside.

Later that afternoon he would be on a plane to the capital, and from there he would fly home tomorrow. Home. He had never thought he would miss New Petersburg, but he did. The "Ridiculous City," as it was called, because of the Media industry and concentration of wealth. Smoggy, tentacular, hyperviolent—and wonderful. Yes. A pang of homesickness hit him. Violet, his wife. His office at Petersburg U . . . Yes, "Ridiculous City" all right: it somehow made you have ridiculous feelings.

Turning away from the window, he picked up the remote and switched on the cable TV. A soap-opera dubbed in Spanish flickered on the grainy screen. Produced in Pete, no doubt. Produced at *home*.

9.

Bailer hated to fly. Especially in old, rusty, military propeller-planes converted into civilian transport by the grace of God and the twisted genius of local mechanics. And if the outside looked bad, the inside was not much better—blue fake-leather 1950s seats, some of them ripped open, showing their yellowed insides. Bailer sat down, sweating and cursing under his breath: the smell of jet fuel pervaded the plane, making him feel dizzy. The only positive thing in all of this was that there were not many passengers. At least he would have a seat to himself.

He watched the luggage trailer roll away. He had his computer and other essential things with him in his small backpack. If his suitcase was stolen, they would only get his dirty clothes.

The engines hiccupped, then gained strength with a terrifying moan. Bailer fastened his seatbelt, watching the jungle move faster past his window. There were three bumps and then the whole thing lifted off with surprising swiftness. They didn't make planes like this anymore, he thought appreciatively.

The sun was slowly setting above the canopy and Bailer began to daydream about the last weeks he had spent here—how he had met Luis, negotiated the hike, and then his encounter with the shaman and Joe M. All of this in the name of science . . . And what had he gotten in the end? His very first drug trip, free of charge, thanks to the Research Committee's grant.

A new Tim Leary.

The thought made him cringe. That was precisely what he wanted to avoid–to be the next drug guru, like Leary, Castaneda or even Huxley. He had read them all and had failed to find any value in their writings. The French poet Michaux was the only one he set aside, because of his near-scientific description of the effects of mescaline and final dismissal of it. His own quest was truly scientific. He wanted to explore Death, if that was possible. The Multiverse theory supported that possibility, and after managing to transfer a few dream images on a computer, he felt that it was time to push his research further.

Ken Kesey's bus was called "Furthur."

Fuck Ken Kesey and his weird spelling.

There was suddenly a shock in the plane, and it dropped a few hundred feet. One woman let out a shill cry and Bailer gasped while a few others laughed nervously. Only an air pocket.

Death. The ultimate mystery. Still.

As a neurophysicist, what he wanted to know was if Death, as a physical place, was only a figment of our imagination, or if it was another dimension, which we accessed through the process of dying. The Land of the Dead. Old, old myths. Mysterious lands, all with a river or water, where your family and friends walked about. A lot of similarities—and a lot of differences—between cultures. He hoped he could show decent results soon, so his grant would be prolonged. Joe M. wasn't one of them.

He had loved the show as a kid, watching it on the Vintage Channel. He liked the detective's suits, his nonchalant air and especially his car, a green Dodge Dart. Thinking back on his hallucinatory experience, Bailer couldn't help wonder at the complexity of the human brain . . . Of course, he had studied dreams and their structure. And even captured some of them on screen. At least, some very blurred images. It had earned him tenure, but the economic prospects had been disappointing. Although he had patented his GreenDreamMachine®, as he had called it, the visual results were too vague to launch it commercially. He didn't care (he actually thought it was a very bad idea to watch your dreams on screen—Wim Wenders had already shot a disappointing movie about that, *Until the End of the World*, which had nonetheless inspired his research, although he had slept through half the film,) but the university's board of trustees had been very disappointed. They had hoped for a great commercial success in order to save some of the humanities departments—unfortunately, it didn't happen.

So, after dreams, death, yes.

Bailer turned his head to look at the clouds through the window and saw the engine burst into flames. He let out a small cry of panic, immediately followed by the other passengers' real screams, as the other motor exploded too.

Death, yes, how ironic, he thought as the plane morphed into an anvil plummeting towards the jungle below. *Shit.*

10.

The smell of salt water and a wet feeling around his thighs woke Bailer up. A fresh breeze lifted his frizzy hair and the lapping around of the waves confused him. The weight of his body seemed incredible. Blinking a couple of times, he wriggled his fingers. At least he wasn't paralyzed from the waist up. He would find out about the rest later, when he would try to stand up. The plane. Where was the plane? And the jungle? Suddenly filled with panic, he sat up on the wet sand. A beach. He was on a beach. Looking down, he realized that his butt was being soaked by the tide. There was also a lot of blood on his shirt. He frantically unbuttoned it and saw an ugly gash on his right side. Strangely, he didn't feel any pain.

A noise made him turn his head. Another passenger was walking on the beach, a little further away. Some people ran to him and hugged him, crying and shouting things in Spanish. More noises. A woman, then another walked past him, towards another group on the beach. More tears, more shouts. Then the pilot and the co-pilot trampled by, leaving deep shoe-prints in the sand. They, too, joined a small assembly.

What about me? Bailer thought. *Why isn't there anybody waiting for me? And where the fuck am I?*

His thoughts gradually clearing, he stood up, watching the strangers leave. His eyes becoming accustomed to the blinding sun,

Bailer saw something that made his heart sink. He recognized it. The city. Farther away, but it was the same city. Joe M.'s city.

As on cue, he heard someone calling him.

"Hey, mister, you're all right?"

Before turning around, he knew who it was.

Joe M. stood beside his car, parked some 50 yards away on the side of the coastal road. He was waving. Bailer feebly waved back and began walking in the detective's direction.

11.

The car was fast and the detective drove it expertly with one hand on the wheel.

"Seems that you and I are bound to meet," Joe M. said, taking his eyes off the road for a few seconds. "Lucky I was driving by. You seem to have arrived here for good now."

"What do you mean?" Bailer asked, confused.

Joe M. tapped briefly on Bailer's stomach.

"The blood. You didn't bleed last time. What happened?"

"The plane, it . . . " Bailer started, then shook his head in disbelief. "I must be in a coma. Talking to myself. You don't exist. Nothing here exists."

Joe M. smiled his famous lopsided smile.

"Heard that one before, many times. You'll get used to it."

"Used to what?"

"You really don't get it, do you?" Joe M. asked, this time obviously amused. "Death, of course. This is the Land of the Dead, the Western Lands or whatever you want to call it."

Bailer didn't know if he wanted to scream, cry or laugh.

"But this is crazy. I'm not dead. I don't *feel* dead."

Joe M. carefully parked the car on the side of the road. He looked thoughtful.

"Hmmm," he said. "Maybe you're not actually dead. Or not yet. It's true that you had no family waiting for you. And I assume that you have lost some of your family, yes?"

Bailer nodded.

"All my grandparents. An aunt, two uncles. A cousin, but I didn't like him . . . And, of course, our little . . . "

"Empty your pockets," Joe M. interrupted him.

"What?"

"Empty your pockets."

Bailer obeyed. Reaching inside his pants, he extracted keys, a used Kleenex and some foreign change.

Joe M. smiled.

"Okay, you're not dead. Yet."

"How do you know?" Bailer asked, still holding his open hand before him.

The P.I. pointed at the objects collected in Bailer's palm.

"When you die, all the objects remain behind. So you're not dead. Same goes in reverse. The Dead can't bring anything from here. Unless they're asked to. And if you come back with something you picked up because you need it, it will follow you. Ok, it's a little complicated, but it's the rules of the Universe. The karmic thing, you know . . ."

Bailer let the words sink in, astounded. He didn't know a coma could be that weird.

"Here, let's have a test," Joe M. said.

The detective took out a small wallet from his jacket's inside pocket and opened it.

"Take this," he said, offering his card. "If you do get back among the living, you'll see I was telling the truth. I'm not supposed to do that, of course, because you don't *really* need it, but I like you. You look like a good guy. Don't ask me why."

Joe M. started the car again. Bailer looked at the card and put it in his shirt pocket.

Whatever, he thought.

And night fell again.

12.

Pain. Excruciating pain. And a strange numbness. The smell of something burning. Screams in Spanish. Hands grabbing him. Horrible pain. Then nothing. Nothing at all.

2. COAST RIDE

1.

JOE M. P.I. slowed down as he exited the freeway and joined the slow traffic moving towards the City. Looking at his watch, he cursed under his breath. This was the Land of the Dead, for Christ's sake! Couldn't they do better than reproduce the L.A. freeways' congestions? Was that what Death was all about? Slowing down? Criminy! Talk about a scam! The dark green Dodge Dart GTS purred down to first gear and Joe M. slammed the driving wheel with both hands. As if he had time to spare . . . Man, when you were dead, it seemed you had even less time than when you were alive.

2.

He finally managed to exit onto the coastal road and speed up. The Boss hated delays as much as Wickersham, his old boss, did at InterCheck, the private detective agency. He had quit then, but how can you quit death? *Good question, sir.* He smiled to himself and admired the ocean view from the corner of his eye.

The endless pale blue sea gnawed at the yellow sands of the beach, everything overlooked by a slightly darker sky. He didn't know if this was Paradise, but from here, in the fast Dodge Dart GTS that never had any mechanical problem and always had a full gas-tank, it sure felt like it.

3.

The Boss lived in a strange ochre and dirty-white stucco villa that looked like a Disneyland castle, perched up on a dark red rock cliff overlooking the sea. The place was surrounded by high, yellow, brick walls, interrupted only by a formidable wrought-iron gate in the middle, painted a somber green. Two winged-monkeys, dressed as bellhops, guarded the entrance. Joe M. hated those monkeys. Looking like mean stuffed animals in their ridiculous costumes, they gave him the creeps. And their eyes . . . Black shiny buttons, darting like quick insects on their fur surrounds. He shivered involuntarily as he stopped the car in front of the villa's walls. The monkeys quickly opened the gates, and he waved at them as he drove on, but they didn't wave back.

4.

The monkey-in-chief was waiting for him at the top of the imposing yellow marble stairs that led to the villa's front door. His uniform was blue, with gold threads. *Even more ridiculous*, Joe M. thought, struggling hard not to show his contempt as he got out of the Dodge Dart. He quickly climbed the steep steps and waited for the monkey to open the door. Sometimes Joe M. wished these monkeys could talk. Hell, they had wings—why shouldn't they talk too? He followed the blue suited animal galloping swiftly in front of him in a maze of corridors. They finally arrived in a large hall, with a huge mirror covering the entire northern wall. The Boss. The monkey tapped on a red leather armchair, indicating that the detective should sit down. Joe M. shook his head.

"I'm fine standing, thanks"

The monkey shrugged and loped towards the door. There it remained rigid like a weird teddy-bear.

The mirror lit up and Joe M. saw himself standing in the middle of the large empty hall. He had wondered many times if there wasn't actually someone observing him from behind a one-way mirror. He liked to imagine a short chubby fellow, with a red nose and rosy cheeks.

"Joe!" the voice said. "Glad you could make it so quickly."

It was hard to figure out where the voice was coming from. It felt like the mirror itself was speaking, which was possible, but weird. *OK, the monkeys had wings and bellhop uniforms*, Joe thought. *Anything goes after that.*

"Sir," Joe acknowledged.

He had visited the Boss a couple of times already, and he knew it was serious. The Boss only called when there was big trouble—like the karma fabric being ripped or the balance of Chaos dangerously tilting.

"As you probably guessed, we have a problem."

Joe nodded and waited.

"Phone calls. Again," the voice said, wearily.

Joe M. nodded again. Contact between the Land of the Living and the Land of the Dead was strictly forbidden, because it disrupted the General Cosmic Pattern, or whatever the Boss called it.

"Pranksters or Do-Gooders?"

Some of the Dead had tried to contact the Land of the Living for as long as the Universe, Multiverse, PolyVerse or whatever you wanted to call it, existed. Many of them just wanted to see their family, friends or lovers and give them a last message. They took the risk, knowing that forced reincarnation would be their punishment if caught—although some judges were lenient and let them choose what they wanted to reincarnate as—generally, an insect with a very short life-span, so they would come back here in no time.

But some of the Dead still had serious issues with the Living and tried to get their revenge on them one way or another. One of the latest trends was to call up the Living on their phones or send messages through their email, pretending they were friends or family. Sometimes they would even manage to plant poltergeists through the lines, in order to reap negative karma vibes for their own pleasure.

Joe M. had already caught a few of those Pranksters. Most of them were bored idiots, or just ambitious jerks who believed in the "Freedom Shores of Divine Bliss" urban legend.

How the rumor started, nobody knew—not even the Boss, or so he claimed. The rumor was that the Land of the Dead was not the terminal place, but only a mere passage to a better place—the Freedom Shores of Divine Bliss, where you would actually become a minor god, of Good or Evil, you wished. In order to do so, you had to reap enough karma points—good or bad—during your stay in the Land of the Dead, and at some stage you would be "chosen" and "transformed." Joe thought it was complete bullshit, but some poor souls never seemed satisfied with what they got and craved for more . . .

Just as the Pranksters existed, there were also secret associations of Do-Gooders that tried to tip their karma the other way—which was just as illegal and dangerous for the whole "General Cosmic Pattern" thing, or GCP, as the Boss called it. They contacted the Living to offer "guidance" and "support," which was usually either inefficient at best or catastrophic at worse. The Do-Gooders' hidden agenda, like the Pranksters', seriously endangered the general picture, at least according to the Boss.

"Pranksters, most probably. And it's very serious this time, Joe. They called up the presidents of the Western Alliance, the Slavic Empire and the Chinese Confederation . . . Even the pope," the boss added, and Joe thought he could detect a smirk in the voice.

"What did they say?" Joe asked.

"The connections were bad—fortunately. But it sounded like advice . . . Crazy advice. They told the Pope he should get married."

It was Joe's turn to smirk.

"You've got to catch them before the whole GCP begins to dislocate . . . From what I've been told, some hacktivists have already posted excerpts of the phone calls and the tabloids are going berserk down there . . . "

Joe nodded. He never questioned his mission. He was a private eye, just doing his job. He had a cool office in the suburbs, a perfect secretary—Daisy—and the Boss gave him enough work to be happy. What the Boss or others believed in was entirely their business. Joe himself had never seen, nor heard, of anyone being "chosen" and "transformed", although the Land of the Dead was way too large for him to know what was going on in other places.

To be honest, he actually liked being dead, even though it got a little too repetitive at times. And the paperwork was a real pain.

"Do you know where those calls came from, Boss?" he asked, taking his notebook out.

The mirror flickered, forming visible words.

"Here is the address. Be careful. I would hate to lose you, Joe."

Violence was not unusual in the Land of the Dead. Many warrior cultures maintained their traditions. The Valkyries still thrived in the icy parts of the Germanic realms and the Saturday Battle Contests were one of its many aspects. But it was symbolic violence, as those "killed" were not destroyed, but merely psychically "knocked-out" for the time of the battle. The same went for "human sacrifices"—Joe M. had to go to the Aztec territories once, and had witnessed one of those mass-murdering ceremonies—although he knew it was all an act, he still had nightmares about it.

What the Boss meant was another kind of violence altogether. Intentional violence with the objective of destroying the individual and sending his soul back into the Samsara whirl, where it would be subject to random reincarnation. The worst of the worst. It was rare, but it did exist, and one had to be careful.

Joe M. jotted the address down, raised his hand to his brow in a mock salute and followed the monkey through the mansion's maze back to the entrance door.

Sitting behind the wheel of his faithful Dodge Dart again, he patted the karmic gun hanging under his left armpit. His best friend, even in death.

5.

Joe M. parked a block away from the address, which was located in the Chinese district. Intense yellows and reds, reflected in the shop windows and car bumpers, caught his eyes as he walked towards the hotel from where the phone calls had been made. The streets were crowded, a tight mixture of tourists and afternoon shoppers. Joe M. loved the smell of Chinatown—exotic, varied, impossible to define— a smell that sometimes made him regret life, one of the nuances that gave the shortness of existence its beauty and frailty. The strength of the moment. The imaginary colors of one's existence. The detective shrugged and straightened his narrow black tie. No time for poetry. This was death, after all. This was serious.

6.

A chubby young man with thick glasses and acne scars sat behind the desk of the Celestial Hotel. He was reading a Chinese newspaper, but put it aside as Joe M. walked into the tiny lobby. Joe M. introduced himself. The boy nodded, and got up.

"The Boss called and told me you'd be coming."

He had a high-pitched voice that didn't match his girth. Here nobody would give it any attention—there were stranger things around—but the detective wondered how it must have been for him when he was alive. Sometimes Death did provide some comfort.

"Can I see your register?"

The boy turned the opened register on the desk towards Joe M. He read Mr and Mrs Universale Salami. Probably not their real names—although he would check anyway.

"What did they look like?"

The fat boy shrugged.

"Normal. I mean, like normal tourists. We get so many customers. I don't pay attention."

"Can you describe them?"

"Well, they looked like Ken and Barbie—you know, the dolls?"

Joe M. nodded.

"He had a nice face, very normal. And she was blonde, very normal too . . . Except for . . . "

He mimed gigantic breasts.

"I see," Joe said.

Ken and Barbie, fabulous.

"I want to see the room," he added.

Joe followed the boy up the stairs to the second floor, and then along an L-shaped corridor to the last door on the left. The place was clean, with reproductions of famous Chinese etchings hanging from the walls. The wall lamps gave out a strange yellow-orange light, turning the shadows into dream-like creatures. The boy opened the door.

"See if you can find anything. I haven't cleaned it yet," the chubby youth said. "You don't have to lock the door when you're finished. I'll do that myself."

Joe M. nodded and the boy walked away. The detective realized he couldn't hear the sound of footsteps. The mysteries of the Orient.

7.

As he stepped in, Joe M. immediately understood why the chubby boy had told him he hadn't cleaned the room yet. The place was a stinking mess; the sheets of the large double-bed had been thrown on the floor, as if a Greek statue had left her garments behind, there were cigarette butts everywhere, emptied bottles of hard liquor scattered around, and a couple of cold "super family" pizza boxes on the small table, uneaten slices peeking out. Mingling with the smell of stale food was the distinct odor of marijuana. *Of course*, Joe thought, *of course*.

Given the state of the room, Joe guessed they were probably Pranksters, although the Ken and Barbie look pointed at Do-Gooders. Of course, the Pranksters were masters of subversion and it would be typical of them to use a Do-Gooders' disguise. Then again, the contrary could be true. Do-Gooders could have trashed this room, so that the Pranksters would be blamed . . .

Hotel room, disguise, multiple possibilities—this wasn't going to be easy. Joe shook his head and sighed. He would have to ask around. Sometimes it was hard to tell Death from Life.

8.

Daisy looked up from behind the huge electric typewriter that almost filled up the entire surface of her desk. She had cut her hair in a smart bob, and she looked even more beautiful than usual. Her deep brown eyes shone under her long lashes as Joe stepped into the P.I. agency's lobby, and her orange turtleneck contrasted beautifully with her dark skin.

"Nice haircut," Joe said.

Daisy flickered her eyebrows and smiled.

"Thank you, Joe. I felt like a change would be welcome."

Joe nodded. There were constantly flirting, but both were too aware of their respective situations to push it any further. Daisy was beautiful, but Joe M. was still her boss. And the age difference didn't help— in Joe's eyes at least. What was more, when Joe M. thought about sex, it was the same way grown-ups thought about playing with toys. They could still picture it in their minds, but would never actually lie down on the floor and smash toy cars together and mimic loud explosions. Maybe they could, if they wanted to, but most of them didn't *really* want to. Still, their mutual unspoken affection created a nice working atmosphere. There was not enough loving in the Land of the Dead, Joe often thought. Indifference, boredom and frustration were the most common traits he encountered. No wonder the Dead had suffered from a bad rep among the Living for centuries.

"I'll be in my office," Joe said, "but I'm incommunicado, ok? Except for the Boss, of course."

"Everything ok, Joe? You look worried. I know those frown lines of yours . . . "

He smiled and shook his head.

"Nah, everything's fine. Just another Prankster phone call situation. Except they really went too far this time—called the pope."

Daisy raised her beautiful eyebrows simultaneously.

"The pope? Oh, Joe . . . "

The P.I. winked at her as he opened the door to his office. *What a lovely person*, he thought. *What a lovely, lovely person.*

3. RESEARCH

1.

BAILER WAS ALMOST finished. He rubbed his eyes with the fingers of his right hand and shut off his laptop. He yawned, stretching on his chair, and winced. His right arm still hurt, especially when he worked too much, and so did his left leg. The study was as quiet as the rest of the house. He looked at his watch. 2A.M. Violet must be sound asleep. She was teaching tomorrow. He grabbed the cane that was resting against the desk and winced again as he rose from his chair.

Souvenirs from South America.

He still had nightmares about the crash. Two years ago. Yesterday. Even after his last year of experimenting and gathering data for his paper, he was still afraid of dying. Man *definitely* wasn't a rational human being.

Yet, he had to admit that Joe M. and the other dead he had encountered in his expeditions hadn't seemed particularly happy. The Land of the Dead actually reminded him of the way the ancient Greeks and Romans saw it—a gigantic empire of boredom. Hell, they had to stage old battles in order to have fun . . . The Athenians against the Spartans, the Prussians against the French, the Americans against the British—every day had its special event. The dead must have felt the dullness of repetition, as they also staged "Special" battles: the Samurai against the Aztecs, The Zulus against the Vikings, the Inuit against the Bushmen . . . And the colors seemed faded, like old wallpaper. Dead boring indeed. He smiled at his own joke. And now he was dead tired. He didn't even try to smile at that one.

2.

Violet snored slightly and didn't wake up as he slid in between the warm sheets next to her. It was a hot August night and they had left the window open. There was a breeze moving the curtains, but it was warm. Lying on his back, he stared at the dark ceiling. If what he had discovered was true, it was amazing. *If.*

Images flashed in the private cinema of his mind. The hospital, where everybody was nice and had treated him very well. He had even gained weight. Dolores, the head nurse, had told him she wanted him to leave the country with a few good memories, so she took extra care of him and made sure he always had excellent food. Luis had come to visit, escorted by He-Who-Has-Six-Eyes. The Shaman had looked at him intensely, and didn't spit this time. He had even smiled a little. Later, when Bailer returned to learn the composition of the sacred beverage, they had become good friends, taking a trip together to the Land of the Dead, where the Shaman had introduced him to his ancestors. They all spat on the ground. It was probably a family thing.

He had gone back to the village twice, staying there two weeks each time. He almost spoke Spanish by then, and his stomach had become accustomed to the spicy food. The last time, an anthropologist, a biochemist and a doctor had come with him. They had tried the drug, but hadn't been convinced. Two had seen the city, but only vaguely, and they hadn't met anybody they knew. Bailer had told them he had had the same impression the first time, but they were unimpressed. They were colleagues from the same university and Bailer knew it was best to remain on good terms, so he didn't start a discussion with them. Leary had tried to convince the world. We all know what happened. The last thing Bailer wanted was the police coming for him at three in the morning.

Knowing that objects could be carried when in a living-dead state, he had taken a small camera with him during the last trip; unfortunately, it had frozen when he came back and the memory card had been ruined. He was really disappointed. There were some good pictures of him and Joe M., taken by He-Who-Has-Six-Eyes.

3.

Violet sighed and moved in her sleep. Her hand fell on his chest, like a warm bird shot down by a hunter. She had been a great support. A school teacher, she only followed his research with a distant eye, although she did tell him she found it fascinating. But she was more interested in her pupils' progress than in the Land of the Dead. Only once she did ask him something, and it was about their daughter. Of course. "Did you see her?"

Bailer had silently shaken his head. She had nodded and had returned her attention to the news. He had felt a darkness pervading his entire body, and had taken her hand. As he was doing now, caressing it like a wounded bird. Emily had died of crib death at the age of one. They had cried and cried, buried her in a little white coffin with one of her teddy bears, and cried and cried again for weeks. They were still crying inside, although the years had reduced the strength and frequency of the tears to the occasional drizzle of an autumn shower.

When Violet had asked him if he had seen their baby girl, he knew she wouldn't understand his answer. Hell, he didn't even know why he hadn't asked Joe M. to find her. Because he was afraid? Because he felt guilty? Because he couldn't go back and leave her all alone in the big city?

The rational situation he had constructed for himself had been: no contact with familiar dead, so that the experiment would remain scientific, untainted by personal data. That was, of course, bullshit.

The real reason for not asking to see his daughter was that he had been scared, terrified even, of the possible answers. "She's not here" would have been the worst. The worst, yes, because where could she have been otherwise?

He had asked Joe M. some fundamental questions about God, Heaven and Hell, but the television P.I. had shrugged them off.

"I have no idea what you're talking about," Joe M had said, looking genuinely surprised.

4.

Bailer had just finished his breakfast and was washing his cup in the sink when his mobile rang. He put down the cup and dried his hands on his pajama pants, wondering who would call him so early during the summer vacations, hoping it wasn't one of his Ph.D. students. It took him a few minutes to locate his phone in the pocket of his pants, discarded on the bedroom floor. By the time he got it out, the ringing had stopped. He let out a sigh of relief when he recognized the number of the missed call: Norman, his friend at the university lab. Bailer had given him some samples to analyze, a few stones and a couple of flowers he'd brought back from the Land of the Dead, as he now officially called it in his mind. After the plane crash, he hadn't been able to find Joe M.'s card anywhere. He had to see if the P.I. was wrong, or if the card had been lost during the rescue. So he had brought back some local souvenirs the last time. Maybe Norman had the results, which would be fantastic, because he might wrap up his article before the beginning of the semester.

He quickly pressed the redial key and Norman picked up immediately.

"Todd?"

"Yes?"

There was an awkward silence on the phone.

"Hmmm, this is going to sound weird . . . "

Todd held his breath. Of course it was going to sound weird. He had brought back some stones and flowers from the Land of the Dead—what was Norman expecting?

"I'm ready," he said and realized his throat was dry.

"Well, I ran the usual routines on the five stones and the three plants you gave me and . . . Well . . . "

"Yes?"

"The results . . . H_2O . . . Only H_2O . . . Water."

"Water?"

"Yes, absolutely pure water—no bacteria. Purest water I ever got to analyze. But that's not all . . . "

Bailer felt his heart beating in his throat.

"Go on."

"They're gone."

"What?"

Norman's laugh sounded like ice cracking.

"Yes. Gone. Evaporated."

Bailer's brain cells went into hyperdrive.

"Did you see that happen?"

"No. But I left the lab to go to the bathroom, and when I came back—nothing. Gone."

"Could somebody have snatched them?"

"No. I worked alone. Besides, who would snatch five little stones and three dead plants?"

There was a pause.

"I don't know what to think," Norman said.

Todd laughed nervously.

"Well, now you know exactly how I feel. Can you forward me the results?"

There was another awkward silence.

"Listen Todd, I don't want you to take it badly, but you have to promise not to mention me in your paper. I . . . I don't want to be considered crazy. Not that I consider you crazy—hell, I saw those stones with my own eyes . . . But the Board . . . You know . . . I can't afford a scandal . . . And frankly, if I were you, I'd be careful with this . . . There are no more hippies around to support you, if you understand what I mean . . . "

"I do, thanks. And don't worry. I won't mention you."

"Thanks."

After Norm hung up, Bailer stared straight ahead, not seeing. Water. The evidence gone. Bad craziness. His paper was going to be fantastic.

4. SOME ENCHANTED EVENING

1.

SHOULD I HELP you tie your bow, dear?"
Fucking bitch. Leave me alone.
George Warren, CEO and founder of the Warren Corporation Inc. looked at himself in the bathroom mirror and saw: an old Jew with white hair, big ears, big nose, pockmarks on his forehead and two generations of money.

He saw: an anti-Semitic cliché.

He saw: himself.

He wasn't even Jewish.

Fuck that shit.

"Dear?"

"No, no, I'm fine!"

Bitch.

Voices bouncing back and forth through the bathroom door. As always. Was loneliness more sublime when you were ridiculously rich?

He looked at himself: Yes. Absolutely.

2.

Edie was magnificent, as usual. Her blonde hair was perfect, rolled-up in an improbable bun, her deep blue eyes efficiently enhanced by subtle makeup, her rosy lips slightly shining with provocative gloss. Her naked shoulders peaked like beautiful hills out of the cream-colored dress and her long legs ended their supple descent in matching pumps. The ideal wife. Of course, of course. She was thirty years younger than him, and to make things worse, she absolutely adored him. When Warren had set his mind on her, he had intended her to be his trophy wife—and what he got was a *real* one. A strange con, if there ever was one. He knew she suffered from the wall he had managed to build between them, but hell, he wasn't going to give into the *feelings* scam. Not that he didn't have feelings—he just wanted to be able to control them.

She turned around when he walked into the room and flashed him a magnificent smile.

"Your bowtie is messed-up, darling. Here, let me do it."

She extended her arms, but he brushed them away with a tight smile.

"We're going to be late," he said. "Fuck them if they have a problem with my bow tie."

They were going to a fashion show. When you saw what people were wearing there, his bowtie actually looked good, all wrinkled and fucked-up as it was.

3.

In the back seat of the limo, leather and all, at a good distance from Edie, Warren could finally enjoy a moment of silence. He loved the night-ride under the sporadic lamp posts *en route* to the city, glittering at the feet of the colony like a broken necklace. He felt the lights brush against his forehead, like cold, motherly, electric hands. Exactly what he needed at this very moment. The future looked grim—and he wasn't thinking about the fashion show. Tom had sent him the latest market figures and projections, and it didn't look good. If they were lucky not to lose money this year, they wouldn't be making profit either. Second year in a row firing people around the world; not good, even if most firing happened in faraway places.

"You all right, darling? You look preoccupied."

Warren waved his wife off, shook his head without looking at her.

He never told her about his business. She had twenty credit cards and no limit. Kept her busy. And happy. Probably.

He quickly turned his head towards her and she smiled, putting her warm hand on his. Yes, very happy. His heart warmed a notch up. Nice kid. He was a lucky bastard, literally.

Warren let his gaze dissolve in the darkness of the highway once more. What bothered him the most was that his favorite branch in the Corporation was the one in the worst shape: Real estate wasn't what it used to be. Too many laws, too many rules, not enough Great Places to build. The new government had shut all the loopholes that had allowed dramatically beautiful constructions in natural reservations—a small market, yes, but oh so lucrative. To make things worse, every day he received desperate messages from movie stars, rock stars, sports stars, political stars asking him to offer them THE ultimate Villa, built in THE ultimate location—yeah, as if. How many potential customers had he lost this year alone? Twenty? Thirty?

He grunted to himself and Edie patted his hand.

"Dear? You're feeling sick?"

"Nothing dear. Just the garlic giving me trouble."

They'd had mussels for dinner, with white wine and garlic. Delicious. But if he was feeling cranky, he always blamed it on the garlic. Perfect defense.

The lights blossomed as they reached the outskirts of Petersburg, making him blink repeatedly. Too many colors, all of a sudden. Too many colors and not enough possibilities.

4.

The fashion show was boring like all fashion shows, but Edie loved it. She gasped numerous times, raising her hand in front of her perfect mouth, whispering continuous *OhmyGodohmyGodoh myGods*, as if some invisible being massaged her most intimate parts. Warren smiled when she smiled, nodded when she nodded, somewhat glad to see her glad. He was maybe a bastard, but he wasn't a *heartless* bastard. He mentally calculated how many thousands this evening would cost him in buying Edie a whole new wardrobe, then decided to relax a little bit and thought about his latest real estate project, a run-down airport near Samarqand which he would transform into a space-tourism base. He already had a major hotel chain interested, and a few private companies had offered their still-potential rocket services. Space, the final real estate frontier.

5.

After the show, Edie went to say hello to a few of her friends, stunning beauties like her who had married other Uncle Scrooges like him. Warren actually knew a few of the bastard husbands, and shared a drink with them at the open bar. Of course, they all wished the others dead, but they all laughed in unison, shaking their heads at each other's bad jokes. It felt like a theatrical drama, and a rather appalling one, but that's the way things were. Bad actors, true psychopaths. Warren smiled to himself and downed his glass of champagne. Tiny bubbles exploded upon his tongue like golden farts. The image suddenly reminded him of an old joke: "If shit was gold, then the poor wouldn't have an asshole." He shared it with his entourage. They laughed heartily.

6.

"I'm going to bed, darling. I'm exhausted . . . "
　　Warren nodded as he hung his wife's coat on the golden coat rack in the hall. She turned to him, waving "goodnight" with her delicate fingers. Watching her slowly climb up the stairs, Warren felt a pang of desire. They didn't often have sex and she was always the one who invited him. He had never cared much for sex—some expensive call-girls had done the trick, literally, before his marriage. It was too intimate, too threatening; it shattered the personal armor he had so carefully built over the years. When they fucked, they always did it fast and in the dark. Edie had nicknamed him "Rabbit George" and although he knew it wasn't a compliment, he also knew she didn't mean to be cruel. She would always stroke his balding head in the darkness, murmuring "Rabbit George" as if she was consoling a child.
　　Shaking his head to chase away this moment of human weakness, Warren decided to check out the newest addition to his collection. That would put him in a good mood and give him nice dreams—it always did.

7.

Helmut was a *panzergrenadier* from the SS Division Wiking, in his Eastern front uniform. He had come earlier this morning and he was beautiful. Warren's hands were shaking a little as he held up the box, freed from its protective wrap. He was a long awaited addition to his Eastern Front army collection, now about 1,000 pieces in total, which made it the most important military action figure collection in the world. Warren had actually employed two experts who scanned all the specialized magazines to find rare or new models. Nothing escaped them. He even had a very rare model of Josef Stalin in his full WWII uniform, complete with samovar and cigarettes.

Warren carefully set the cardboard box in its reserved space, next to the other members of the German SS divisions, and took three steps back to admire his wall.

Edie thought this was very cute. She even listened to him when he explained what made such and such figure rare, like a left-handed soldier, or a wounded officer. She said he had remained a little boy at heart, which was utter bullshit, but sweet nonetheless.

No little boy could afford such a collection.

8.

On his way to bed, George caught a glimpse of the financial papers scattered on the coffee table. Things looked grim for the real estate business. He had to find something new, something even better than a spaceport. Shrugging, he set his thoughts on Helmut, in his fantastic uniform. He couldn't suppress the first smile of the day, thinking of the wonderful dreams he was going to have.

5. A BUST

JOE M. MOVED cautiously in the hallway, glancing at the apartment numbers as he shuffled along. If his informant was telling the truth, the Pranksters he was looking for were now living in this cozy seashore building. A surprisingly petit-bourgeois place, the detective thought, although it was true that most revolutionaries did come from a middle-class background, when they were not downright nobility, like Kropotkin, for a famous example. Then again, there were no slums in this city. This was the Land of the Dead, after all.

Arriving in front of the number 12, he stopped, carefully listening at the door. Rock music was blasting out on the other side. What a surprise. Joe M. had to think the whole thing through once again. The hotel owner had recognized them on the pictures he had been shown. The mediumic fluid samples matched. It was as simple as that. The pope! They had some guts, he had to admit. Couldn't help smiling in spite of himself. The detective lifted his hand and paused. The poor idiots risked karmic punishment, with a possible reincarnation sentence—heavy, heavy stuff for just a prank. After all, kids would always be kids, even in the Land of the Dead. And radical kids—well, radical kids. He knew that Daisy disapproved of this side of his job. She thought it was harmless jokes and that the karmic laws were stupid and should be changed. He couldn't say he disagreed, but the Boss was the Boss and the laws were the laws. End of the story.

He knocked hard and waited. Nothing. The music kept on tearing the room apart on the other side. He pounded again and this time he heard the music being turned down. The door opened slowly and a beautiful face appeared, looking at him with a mix of candor and provocation. Nancy Custer. He hadn't been really surprised when the hotel guy had pointed at her picture.

"Yes?"

"Who is it?" a man's voice shouted in the background.

Joe recognized the voice. Jeffrey Ruben. The pimply guy had pointed at him too. And the mediumic fluids were a match. Too easy. Too stupid. As if to confirm the P.I.'s thoughts, his face appeared right above the girl's. They both looked completely stoned.

"Ah, the fuzz," Jeffrey said.

"May I come in?" Joe M. asked.

Jeffrey gently pushed Nancy aside and opened the door.

"Sure, man. Come right on in."

Joe M. made his way into the apartment, brushing past Nancy who stared at him with no sign of recognition. He'd already arrested them in the past, for organizing an expedition to the forbidden zone, which was where the shamanic people lived. The zone wasn't really "forbidden," but the use or import of the plants they used in their rituals was. Of course, many citizens disobeyed, pretending to go on tourist trips. Jeff and Nancy had arranged such a tour, with the help of drug guru Trent McKenzie. The result had been a massive drug orgy, with numerous tales of "pre-Death experiences." Although the whole thing had been carefully prepared, Jeff and the others had not planned that the participants would spread rumors about the fantastic trip and even publish accounts in books and magazines. Joe M. had been sent to arrest them as they were preparing a second expedition. The Boss had sentenced them to karma degradation, as a first warning. He wouldn't be so lenient a second time, even for what Joe M. considered a childish prank.

Joe M. sniffed the air and Nancy shrugged, looking innocent. Jeff lifted his chin and pointed at a small statue of Buddha with a bird perched on his shoulder. The ceramic bird held a thick incense stick in its beak. Joe smiled.

"Must be a pretty stoned bird, smoking that kind of stick," he said.

It was Jeff's turn to shrug.

"What do you want, pig?" he asked defiantly.

Joe looked straight at him, but Jeff didn't look down.

"I've got a warrant," he said. "You called the pope and a few others in La-La Land from the Celestial Hotel downtown. I've got plenty of witnesses and we've got a match on the mediumic fluid analysis."

Jeff's eyes narrowed and Joe felt his gun weigh heavier under his armpit. He hoped it wouldn't come to that and was relieved when he saw Jeff throw his hands up in the air.

"It was joke, man. A prank!"

The P.I.nodded.

"I know, Jeff. But the Boss isn't amused. Not a bit."

"A joke, for Christ's sake!"

"Seemed to have caused some disruptions in the Karmic balance. Serious stuff."

"Karmic balance is a myth." It was Nancy's turn to speak. She was amazingly articulate given her hazy look. "It's a myth invented by the authorities in order to keep us oppressed. We want to prove it's bullshit. Bullshit, man!"

Joe M. sighed and produced the Karmic handcuffs from his pocket.

"Bullshit, man," Nancy repeated, offering her wrists. "Pure bullshit."

6. HARD TIMES

PROF BAILER LOOKED at his sorry collection of new students and barely repressed a sigh. There were only five of them, and they all looked weird. Four guys, one girl. One of the guys had glasses so thick his eyes looked like tiny dots and he wore an "I Want To believe" t-shirt. One looked like a sumo-wrestler with a stern look. *Perhaps the only real student*, Bailer thought. The two others were like a pair of New-Age hippies, with strange colors in their hair and slightly off-centered gazes, as if they were on something—which they probably were. The girl was a Goth, with jet-black dyed hair, a pierced nose and dressed all in funeral black.

Five students. Last year, he had twenty-three. Neurophysics was the hot stuff, along with nanochemical engineering and quantum dialectics. He could have asked himself: *What the hell was going on?* but he knew very well what the hell was going on. Himself.

His own sorry self.

Incredibly enough, he had actually managed to single-handedly sabotage his career. He had thought his findings about the Land of the Dead, as he liked to call it, would make a terrific splash in the scientific community, but they had just made a sorry ripple. Of course, he should have known. The *Neurophysics Journal* had been reluctant to publish his findings, and had done so with a statement disclaiming any endorsement on their part. What's more, in their next number, they had prominently published damning criticisms of his findings by major researchers, although Bailer knew that Prof. Scott Rogers, from Babylon Open University, Tarek Khair from New Mumbai University and Prof. Kris Saks, from the Port Moresby Scientific College had sent papers to the *Journal* in his defence.

And of course, ironically, and maybe more tragically, his article had soon been noticed on the Web and had turned him overnight into a counter-culture figure. His worst nightmare had become a sorry reality. The "Death Teacher," as he was now nicknamed, was a Web star of the weird and unorthodox. He had been forced to change his email address because of all the weird shit he received. Two television programs had invited him to become a host. He could have been rich now if he had accepted. Rich, famous and ridiculous. The problem was that Bailer took his research seriously—this wasn't some crackpot theory, this was scientific fact: The Land of the Dead did exist physically and could even be mapped, something traditional Shaman cultures seem to have known for centuries— although it was hard to define on what plane, as he whole-heartedly admitted in the introduction to his article. The fact that it was made of H_2O did pose a problem—but then again, it could be the passage from one plane to another which modified the biochemical components, although living things didn't seem to be altered. Yes, he admitted there were still a great number of questions that remained unanswered, but he had also written that this was the first phase of a deeper and more thorough study.

Which would never happen now, alas, he thought to himself as he spread his notes on the desk in the classroom. The Petersburg University Scientific Committee had barred him from all research funds, arguing that he was giving the establishment a bad name. A good thing he had tenure. Otherwise, he would have been sacked on the spot, no doubt. None of his colleagues talked to him anymore and he had to teach to just five sorry students.

"The brain is an exceptionally complex topic," he began after clearing his throat, "as it is both an organ and a concept. Because of this, I . . . "

One of the students, the Sumo wrestler, raised a hand.

"Yes?"

"Professor, before you talk about the brain, can you tell us about the death place?"

7. SCIENCE TODAY

THINGS HAPPEN BY chance. Always. Being born rich: chance. Good deals: chance. Good wife: chance. Nothing planned, nor predictable here. George Warren killed his cigar in a tiny silver ashtray and took out his bathrobe. He felt the water with the tips of his fingers. Perfect. Chance. Nothing but chance. Everything had been so predictable recently—the market's plunge, the drying-out of possibilities, the end of original projects . . . OK, his space-hotel project was somewhat original, but nonetheless *so* predictable. It didn't take a genius to imagine it. Only good market research. He had to face it: the world had run out of chance. It had become boring. He didn't like it. Not a bit.

Naked and frowning, he picked up the latest issue of *Science Today* he had brought into the bathroom with him and carefully immersed himself into the warm water, holding his right arm up not to wet the magazine. He loved science, although he didn't understand half of what he read. The poetry, the uncertainty of it all—almost comical at times. The reality we lived in—relative. The laws of the universe—relative. The origins of life—relative. That's how he looked at the world: relative. Edie couldn't understand this. Especially when the business was bad. She would flip, he would smile and wait. He knew things would be good again, relatively. No need to panic. Generally, he would write her a big check so she could see he really wasn't worried. Yes, everything was relative. Except Edie's love. Stupid cow. Beautiful, though. Beautiful.

Grunting, he opened the magazine and scanned the collection of short articles on page four. One of them grabbed his attention: "Scientist Claims the Land of the Dead Is a Real Land." He began to laugh out loud, then something made him read it attentively. *Chance*, he thought as his brain began to whirr, *chance*.

2. SODIUM WHITE

1. COLUMBUS

1.

STANDING ON A windy hill overlooking the beach, Joe M. watched the men in blue overalls and yellow helmets through his small, folding binoculars. He had parked his Dodge by the side of the road, killing the engine. There were eight of them, trotting beside the ocean with measuring instruments and what looked to him like large bags of flour or cement. One of the men seemed to hold a small camcorder. They were talking to each other, indicating things that the detective couldn't see. At first, Joe had thought they were just newcomers, victims of some work accident. It wouldn't have been the first time, surely wouldn't be the last. Then he had noticed the bags, and they had intrigued him.

He had been driving to work, but had decided to exit to join route 70 because the 101 freeway was jammed, as usual. The 70 took longer, but what it lost in minutes, it gained in scenery. As far as he knew, he had no appointment this morning, so he drove slowly, taking the landscape in. And that's how he had first noticed them.

Joe lowered the binoculars and rubbed his eyes, then frowned. Something was wrong. He didn't really know what it was, but he knew these eight men shouldn't be there. He had a gut feeling, a hunch, and it said "bad news." Of course, he could have been wrong. Maybe they weren't dead and that's why they had brought their bags with them. But why would that happen? It would have been a first, at least since he had himself arrived in the Land of the Dead.

When he saw one of them open his bag and begin to spread some white powder on the sand, he decided to go have a talk with them. He folded his binoculars, put them in the inner pocket of his jacket and patted his gun. Time for some improvised detective work. The best kind there was.

2.

Joe M. carefully slid down the dried grass slope and began to jog towards the group of workers, who were now spreading the white powder on the beach as they slowly advanced towards another hill further to the east. If they had noticed the detective, they didn't show it and they seemed very concentrated on their work. As he neared them, Joe saw the "boss" tap on his watch and yell something to the others, who looked up and nodded. The detective was just within shouting distance when suddenly the eight men disappeared, with their gear and bags. All that was left was a large circle of shiny white powder.

Joe M. jogged to the spot and looked around, confused. They must have been alive. Or not entirely dead. An occasional shaming coming to visit with ancestors and consult with them was routine, but it became very odd when it involved eight men dressed as construction workers. Joe M. shook his head and tried to step over the white line on the ground, but an invisible force blocked his move, making him momentarily lose his balance.

Frowning, he tried again, but an incredible pain shot through his leg, as if he had rubbed it against a white-hot metal surface. He fell on his ass and quickly lifted his pants' leg over his ankle and calf. His skin was chafed and reddened, as if it had been sprinkled with boiling water. Getting back up, he took out his mobile phone and dialed the Boss's number. Things were more than strange, now. They were frightening.

2.

The police car arrived half an hour after Joe's call. Commissioner Margot got out and walked towards the detective, followed by Gomez, the lab guy. They shook hands briefly.

"So, Joe, where is it?"

"This way. Follow me."

They silently walked side by side the 300 meters to the site.

"There you go. Don't try to walk over the line. I did and . . . "

The detective briefly flashed his leg to Margot, who winced sympathetically.

Gomez pulled on his pants and crouched to examine the scintillating powder.

He looked at it carefully for a few minutes, scrutinizing from various angles. When he stood up again, his face was tense.

"Salt," he said. "It must be salt."

"Salt?" Joe M. echoed. "What's that?"

"Sodium chloride. The ultimate weapon. Totally forbidden in the Land of the Dead. Look."

The detective looked down and frowned with surprise. It was as if the ground had been attacked by some sort of acid. On each side of the long white streak the sand had crystallized, and farther up, on the zone where the beach gradually gave way to grassy patches, the earth and grass seemed to have turned to ash.

"Who would do that?" Joe M. asked aloud, mostly to himself.

Margot shook his head.

"I don't know, but it's bad news. I'm going to call the Boss and set a surveillance team twenty-four-seven. Thanks for calling me."

"Sure," the detective said with a tense smile. "Sure."

Before walking back to his car with Gomez, Margot turned around.

"And, ummm . . . Not a word about this to anybody. I don't want to start a panic."

"Of course."

A hand shielding his eyes, Joe M. watched the car slowly drive back onto the coastal road. Then he remembered that Daisy must be waiting for him at the office, probably worrying. He took out his cell phone to call her. As the Commissioner had said, there was no reason to start a panic.

2. THANATOS CONSTRUCTIONS.

1.

ENTERING HIS BRAND new lab, Todd Bailer couldn't help wondering how this was possible. Did Fate really exist? Was he born under a lucky star? Well, sort of? He had been recruited by the Warren Corporation about seven months ago, and still couldn't believe his luck. Unlimited funding, a brand new lab and capable assistants. He would never have imagined that a real estate corporation would be so interested in the Land of the Dead.

Of course, he had to be careful. Violet, always the revolutionary, had asked him to think twice before accepting a deal with a company she considered a corporate devil. And she was right, of course. But the prospect of finishing his days in a near empty classroom, with no funding for his research and being treated like a hippie guru, was too horrible to face. He had signed his contract with relief, and even joy, although he had told Violet it had been an excruciating moment for him.

From the way she still occasionally left the newspaper opened at articles denouncing the Warren Corporation's evil deeds, he had a feeling she hadn't really believed him. She never said a word about his work, but her silence was more than revealing. Still, she was happy not having a completely depressed husband at home. Or at least she should have been.. Shrugging his thoughts off, he focused on the figures lining up on the screen. Someone entered the room and Bailer greeted him without turning around.

"Hey, Bob! How are things today?"

Bob Stark crossed the lab and peeked at the screen above Bailer's shoulder. His assistant was a remarkable Ph.D student who worked on self-generated archetypal imagery in computer data. A tall young man with a receding hairline and deep black eyes, he had a constant smirk that got on the nerves of most of the staff. His collection of tribal tattoos—mostly collected during his treks in the Samoan Islands where he also studied traditional music as a hobby—didn't help either, especially the one that covered half his face. But it didn't bother Bailer in the least—he actually liked it. It was like working with a mean-looking, savage Mona Lisa. Looking back at his years at the university, he realized how conventional his students had been. Even the oddest ones. This was another league altogether. And he strangely felt at home.

"Looking good, looking good. I think we're ready to go."

Bailer nodded and took a deep breath. He always felt nervous when they were sending a team "over the rainbow", as they called it in their own coded language. So far everything had been going well and that was exactly when you had to be extra careful.

2.

Through the protective-glass window, Bailer looked at the eight sleeping men lying on the narrow beds. Each had an IV pouch dangling over him, its tube trailing like a thin translucent vine, and each had a monitor at the foot of his bed. There was also a pile of salt bags, wrapped up in a transparent blue tarpaulin, its surface shiny with a sticky substance. Two medics in sterile suits walked back and forth, taking notes. Bailer had thought the suits were a little too much: could there really be germs in the Land of the Dead? According to all the data he had gathered, it was constituted mostly of ultra pure H_2O—a mystery that still remained to be explained—but later. The Warren Corporation didn't give a damn about mysteries; they wanted results. And so far, they couldn't complain.

Bailer had never met George Warren, not even when he had signed the contract. Warren's three lawyers had been present though, young clones of the Perfect Lawyer Dressed In A Suit, cramming the small office like smiling wax mannequins. The ink in the Montblanc fountain pen had been black, not red. He'd checked.

"I have them on the radar!" Bob yelled from behind a huge console.

Bailer sighed with relief.

Another person walked in. Spector, the head architect. He recognized her expensive perfume before he saw her. The tap-tap of her high heels was also an easy give away. Bailer heard other steps. Her assistants.

Spector peeked over his shoulder.

"Everything all right?"

Bailer nodded, still looking at the figures on the screen.

"We should get visual contact in a—ah, here it is . . . "

They both turned to look at the other monitor. A shaky image appeared. Seven blue silhouettes standing on a beach. You couldn't see the eighth, who was holding the camera. They all looked like grainy ghosts in a bad Eighties movie.

"Too bad we can't speak to them," Spector said.

The two assistants nodded in unison, a balding young guy with fashionably Bohemian clothes and a middle-aged woman with a jet-black dyed Lulu bob, wearing what looked like a black ninja drag without the funny scarf around the head.

"The memory cards get erased during their return," Bailer patiently explained for the umpteenth time. "We can only have 'live' images."

"And we cannot communicate with them," Spector added.

"Well, technically, they're dead." Bailer explained again. "You can't communicate with the dead here."

"I know people who have," Spector replied dryly.

Bailer shrugged.

"Yes, ok, it might be possible in certain circumstances . . . But technically, radio waves do not cross over . . . We've tried, but it just doesn't work."

"Whatever you say," the architect snorted. "I can see they're working well."

She signaled with her hand to the young male assistant, who handed her a leather rucksack. She took out a poster protection case and pulled out an A2 piece of paper, which she flattened on the table. It was a map of the area where the first villa should stand.

"Yes, they're almost finished isolating the area. We're right on schedule. Warren will be very happy."

She looked at the screen again, and her assistants gathered around her.

"See, over there? Next to the hill? There's a flat patch that will be perfect for the mansion . . . The view from there will be prodigious. Let me show you the latest version. I have worked on it yesterday . . . "

She pulled another sheet of paper from the poster case. Bailer glanced away from the screen and took a peek. It was an architect's drawing, with "THANATOS CONSTRUCTIONS INC." printed in huge letters at the top. Spector studied the drawing, explaining technical modifications to her assistants who nodded in unison.

Bailer was glad he hadn't told Violet anything about this crazy project. She would have flipped—and he wouldn't really have blamed her for that. He wasn't far from flipping himself.

3. NIGHT BLUE

1. MAXIMUM BOUZOUKI

1.

STAVROS WAS ALMOST deserted, but it was still early and it was a Tuesday. Bailer had worked as a waiter while attending college and he knew how dull weeknights could be. He pulled Violet's chair for her while Costa, the indestructible elderly waiter, waited patiently with the menus and with his eternal Hellenic gray mustached smile.

It seemed eons since they had gone to a restaurant—the last time had been six months ago, for their wedding anniversary. Twenty-one years and not a single regret, at least on his part. Tonight was to celebrate the promotion of the Thanatos Constructions Project Inc. structure. He was Senior Researcher now, and that meant a good raise too.

Violet had been reluctant to celebrate at first. Of course, she was happy for him—she loved him, goddammit. But the Warren Corporation still gave her political allergies. To her, it was as if Todd had agreed to work for the Nazis or the KGB, something deeply unethical that her liberal soul couldn't accept. After all, as a teacher, she represented free access to culture, profit-free openness and accessibility, the utopia of global knowledge and equal chances. The Warren Corporation was exactly the opposite. Of course, she knew she was being naïve—it was far more complex than that. The Warren Corporation was also known for its charity programs, and Warren himself had given the city a beautiful museum of contemporary art. But to Violet, this was only an alibi, a public disguise; behind the "do-good" varnish, the Corporate Beast sneered, ready to huff and puff on the poor citizens' cardboard lives. Still, she loved Todd more than anything else in the world, and if he was happy, she would be happy too. Even if he was a fucking social traitor.

2.

Todd Bailer raised his chilled glass of Retsina wine—the best of the house, which didn't mean much—and smiled at his beautiful wife. The alcohol had reddened her cheeks, giving her the colors she sometimes lacked in everyday life.

"To my beautiful wife," he said.

She smiled and they toasted. Putting down her glass, she frowned, as she always did when she suddenly thought of something, "Darling, you never really explained to me what you were doing for the Warren Corporation . . . They're mostly in real estate."

Todd Bailer had another quick sip of his wine. The bottle was half empty and he was already feeling flushed too.

"Well, I did tell you before: I am doing research for them . . . "

"What kind of research? That's what I mean. You're a neurophysicist, Todd. What is that you're doing for them? What do they want from you?"

"Well, as you know, it's a huge corporation. They have a lot of different branches . . . I work for a division called Thanatos Constructions . . . It's focused on that Land of the Dead I was working on before . . . "

Violet shook her head, with an ironic half-smile.

"Thanatos Constructions, yes, I remember you telling me something about it. So, what's the big project? Constructing corporate skyscrapers for the dead?"

Bailer felt himself turn pale in the restaurant's cozy penumbra. She was dangerously close to the truth and he had signed a non-disclosure agreement along with the contract. If they found out he had given her the name of the division they would fire him. Or murder him. Or her. Or both. At least.

"It's not the real name, I just made it up," he quickly answered. "You know I can't tell you anything about it. Top secret."

Violet looked at him with suspicion in her eyes.

"You're not working on some secret weapon project, are you?"

Bailer felt temporarily relieved. She was now heading in the wrong direction. Excellent.

"No, no I swear! I would never do that. I do have some ethics, you know!"

He took her hand between his. She tilted her head to one side and scrutinized him.

"I love you," she said.

"I love you too," he said, meaning it with all his heart.

It was her turn to lift her glass. He leant over his half-finished lamb with Greek potatoes to kiss her, when music suddenly crashed into the room, full blast. A young musician he hadn't noticed now stood behind a huge electronic keyboard in the corner of the restaurant, wearing a blood-red shirt, his drawn-back hair glistening with grease.

"Maximum bouzouki!" he screamed into the mike, his voice louder than the heart-stopping melody. "Let's go! Let's go!"

The waiter approached their table with the dessert menu.

"My cousin," he said, indicating the musician with a sharp tilt of his head. "Very talented."

2.DINNER FOR TWO

1.

DAISY HAD BEEN surprised but she had accepted the date. The last couple of weeks had been extremely busy because of the situation on South West Beach, and Joe M. felt like he should show his favorite secretary some appreciation ... and even a little more than that, although he still felt awkward acknowledging his own feelings. There had been this new disease— if one could call it that in the Land of the Dead, where such things seemed impossible—which gave people the incredible urge to fornicate, and Joe M. didn't want Daisy to misunderstand him. The disease had spread incredibly fast, and shocking scenes occurred every day. It could happen anywhere; in the streets, at the library, in this restaurant. Nobody knew what was happening, but Joe M. had his little theory, which he had shared with the Boss. He thought it was somewhat related to the South Beach situation, and the Boss agreed with him. Of course, he couldn't prove anything yet, but time and the police lab results would tell.

The waiter appeared, interrupting his thoughts. He showed the detective a bottle of Saint-Emilion. Joe nodded.

"Oh Joe, this is so nice of you," Daisy sighed as the waiter poured wine into their glasses.

Joe M. vaguely remembered when he used to eat and drink because he needed to. Another heavy dependence of the Living. Now, it was only for the pleasure of taste, like going to see a wonderful movie or visiting a gallery to see van Gogh's latest paintings.

"I can't thank you enough for your fantastic help, Daisy," Joe said, lifting his glass. "You're a wonderful, wonderful woman."

Daisy lowered her eyes, visibly moved, then looked up again and smiled.

"And you are a wonderful boss," she said.

Joe's heart winced at the word. He wished she would have said "man" or even "person" instead of "boss."

The conversation drifted towards their everyday topics—friends, families, cases. She was wonderful. He wished they could live together. What a wonderful companion she would make.

As if she could read his thoughts, Daisy asked him how his search for a new home was going. He had told her that he was getting tired of his flat and was thinking of moving closer to the beach, possibly in a house.

"Nothing definite," he said, smiling and shaking his head. "Haven't found anything suitable yet. And with this trouble on South West Beach, I don't really feel like looking around."

"Yes, of course, I understand," Daisy said. "It would drive anybody crazy—all that commotion."

"Yes. It would."

He felt like telling her "Let's find a flat together and move in, like crazy young lovers! You're the woman of my life!" Or rather, "You're the woman of my Death!" but he just kept nodding, trying to think of something else to talk about. He was starting to worry, all of a sudden. Could he be smitten too?

2.

"Thank you for a wonderful evening," Daisy said as they reached the door of her small house in the North-West quarter, a nice residential area with beautiful gardens. *She smells as good as her flowers*, Joe M. thought.

"My pleasure," he answered, moving a little closer.

She rummaged in her handbag, looking for her keys. When she found them, she leaned forward and kissed him on the cheek.

"Now, be a good boy and go straight home. We've got a long work day tomorrow!"

The contact of her full lips on his rugged flesh sent tiny sparks of pleasure down to his heart. He felt like grabbing her by the shoulders and giving her a full-mouthed kiss right here, right now, but something in him managed to resist. *Once a gentleman, always a gentleman*, he thought, walking back to the Dodge Dart. *Alas*.

3.

Turning the half-empty glass of whisky between his hands under the bar's yellow spotlight, Joe M. sighed to himself and took a long sip. Sharkey's was quiet tonight and he was sitting alone at the counter. Perfect. He felt like a fool and didn't want to make small-talk with anyone. *Love is indeed eternal*, he thought, putting down the glass. The ice-cubes clinked ironically. *And that really sucks*.

3. THIRTIES CHARISMA

1.

WARREN WAS EXHAUSTED and the last thing he wanted was to go out. But Edie had told him she had reserved a table at this brand new place that served amazing burgers, and she knew he was a sucker for authentic home-made cheeseburgers. Unfortunately, there were not that many good authentic burger joints left in this city, so he was willing to give it a try. Edie had good taste in food, he had to give her that. She had made him invest in a few good places in town and all across the universe. Never had to complain. He had even created a new division in the Warren Corporation, Warren Foods Inc. *So lucky*. He smiled at his reflection in the limo's ark window. *So fucking lucky, so fucking rich, you fucking bastard.*

2.

The Maître D' welcomed him and led him to a table in a private space in the back of the restaurant, which was decorated like a thirties' art deco upper-class joint. The furniture looked genuine. It must have cost a fortune, and the effect was striking. One had the feeling that Hemingway or Fitzgerald could walk in any minute, drunk, disheveled and lost. He hated to admit it, but at first glance he loved it. The period's style implied something wonderfully creepy for him: beautiful straight lines before catastrophe and chaos. It deeply moved him. He spotted Edie at the table. She waved at him as soon as she saw him. There were two martini glasses on the table. Perfection was absolute.

3.

"How do you like this place, darling?" Edie asked him after he sat down.

He didn't want her to think she had hit one of his soft spots, so he just shrugged.

"Looks okay so far," he mumbled.

But he couldn't help taking her hand and lifting it to his lips. A stupid reflex, which he immediately regretted.

"Wait until you taste their cheeseburgers," Edie said, winking. "But first . . . "

She bent down to pick something up from under the table and put it on his plate, with a big grin on her face. A present.

"What the fuck?" Warren asked, completely taken by surprise.

"Happy birthday, darling!"

Warren felt himself on the verge of blushing. His birthday. Fucking shit. What now? She had fortunately forgotten to bring the little paper hats and the cupcakes.

He forced a smile and began to unwrap the package, which was the size of a shoebox. As the present was revealed, Warren had the sudden embarrassing feeling that he was reliving a childhood scene: he, under the Christmas tree, surrounded by Mother and Father, discovering the electric train set he had wished for. It was the one and only time they had actually bought him something from his wish-list, and later that day Mother told him they had done so because they had to tell him that Father had terminal phase cancer. Warren's fingers began to slightly tremble as he freed the package from its paper shroud.

"Adolf, the WWI infantryman!" he gasped, feeling ridiculous tears sting the corner of his eyes. "How did you . . . How could . . . ?"

Edie was all smiles, her own eyes shiny with tears.

"Look!" Warren squealed, almost out of himself. "There is even the Iron Cross for Outstanding Duty!"

If Edie had asked him to put her on his will that very moment, he would have without any hesitation. Fortunately for him, she didn't. Later, on the way back to their mansion, sitting with her in the back of the limo where she was giving him his second birthday present, he shivered retrospectively.

4. TROUBLE PURPLE

1. SAND CASTLE

1.

SPECTOR LOOKED AT the beach and the surrounding landscape, ignoring the mesh of police cars and media trucks surrounding the site. Bailer stopped right behind her, feeling nervous. He had only agreed to come because he was curious to see what was going on with his own eyes instead of on a screen, but he resented being here. In some very eerie way, he felt like they were trespassing. If Violet had been present, she would have filed for divorce without a second thought.

Spector's female assistant turned to her male colleague.

"They have cops in heaven?" she chortled.

"Trouble in Paradise," joked the young man.

Bailer, who stood next to them, couldn't help reacting.

"Technically, this isn't Heaven. It's the Land of the Dead and . . ."

"Yeah, whatever," the old Lulu said. "They still have cops."

Spector resumed her walk towards the huge villa that was standing on the hill. Although it was only half-finished, it was still spectacular. A mixture of Bauhaus and ultra-modern lines, Bailer thought, although he knew absolutely nothing about architecture. If he had been a dying billionaire, he would have bought it immediately.

The inside was even more impressive, although the walls were still unpainted and the furniture hadn't yet been installed. Spector and her assistants, followed by the various construction engineers, charged through the rooms, talking about "moods," "effects" and "wellness after death." Bailer heard their steps echo in the empty rooms and a feeling of doom suddenly overwhelmed him.

What was he doing here? What had this to do with his original research, with its purpose, which was, after all, only to prove that the Land of the Dead was as material as our Earth, in another plane or dimension? He had proven his point, and too bad for the unhappy consequences . . . Oh the Shakespearian, Marlovian, Goethean, whatever, pride! *Alas, poor Faust* . . . Exactly. But it was too late, and he couldn't quit now, as he didn't want to end up in jail, or worse, for contract breaching. You only had one life, after all.

2.

He was a traitor. To what exactly, he didn't really know, but he knew he was. Staring at the dark ceiling, he sighed as silently as possible, not wanting to wake Violet up. His thoughts drifted to Emily and he felt a big emptiness, like a warm, soft and half-deflated birthday balloon. Normally, he would shut himself up, lock the door to that terrible morning, the now useless toys, the happy baby pictures . . . but tonight he wanted to face her, hold her frail one-year-old-body against him and tell her that he loved her. The Land of the Dead. Yes. Why hadn't he seen her? Why hadn't he seen any of his family or friends; like Thomas, who had died in a booze-related accident when they were students? Or Oliver, who had committed suicide? He'd seen only strangers. Nice strangers, like that man, Joe, whom he had seen and small talked with a couple times, the detective from that TV series of his childhood . . . But strangers nonetheless.

Sometimes he wondered if he hadn't taken too much of that drug the first time he had been with the Shaman, and that he was, in fact, in a coma, imagining all this. But Violet turned in her sleep, snoring discreetly like the teacher she was, and he cuddled against her, hoping the darkness would engulf him.

2. ACTION AND REACTION

1.

JOE M. LOOKED THROUGH his binoculars at the small group entering the half-finished house or building or whatever that monstrosity was. He felt like an Apache in old westerns looking at the arrival of new wagons in the canyon. Hell, he was an Apache and they were indeed colonists. No other explanation for this mess. The cops were watching too, standing beside their cars, lights flashing like demented pinball machines. Nothing they could do, and their frustration was perceivable through their body language, from here. Tense shoulders, tightened jaws, ironic sneers. But the salt barrier made it impossible for them to interfere. It could kill you in a moment if you tried to touch it. The Boss had warned everyone and there were big signs all around with drawings to explain the dangers. The area had been quarantined to prevent onlookers from doing the stupid things onlookers generally do, like trying to take back a souvenir. *"Hey, where's my hand, dude?"* Exactly. Didn't want that to happen. Bad for the general Karma, as the Boss would say. Joe still had a nasty scar where he had been burned. The hairs had just begun to grow back and he was happy he never wore shorts.

A face in the group suddenly registered. He knew he had seen it before. Joe's mind raced, looking for a memory lost in one of its millions of pockets. Then, he remembered: it was the visitor he had encountered a couple of times on the same shore, north of here. He was a professor, named Todd Bailer if he remembered correctly, who had mistaken him for someone else at first. He had asked a few questions about the Land of the Dead, but had never stayed long. Joe had run into him by chance once or twice, exchanged a few words. A curious visitor. He thought he had seen Bailer once with one of the numerous shamans who visited the wild plains of the west, but he wasn't sure. Joe had been driving full speed on the main road, coming back from a quick check on a possible psychotropic mushroom traffic ring in the region which proved to be just a group of friends having a picnic. What was Bailer's role in this? Why was he here with *them*? The real mystery. The solution also, perhaps. He had to find out. He put away the binoculars and took out his camera. Fiddling with the heavy zoom, he took a series of pictures.

2.

Daisy took the memory card in her hand, with question marks in her beautiful brown eyes.

"Some pictures I took at the beach. I want to see if the Boss can identify one of the intruders . . . "

Daisy nodded and inserted the card into the desk computer to download the pictures onto the hard-disk. Before forwarding them to the Boss, she turned around, frowning as if a thought hung heavy on her brow.

"I wanted to tell you . . . I really enjoyed dinner with you, the other night. Thank you."

Joe M. cleared his throat and smiled defensively.

"Me too. We should do it again some time."

He wanted to say *every night*, but she had already turned away and was now looking at the screen. Joe went into his office and gently closed the door. He sat down, took a deep breath, and shook his head. To be a teenager for eternity—and people wondered if Hell existed?

3.

"A scientist?"

"That's what our files say. Todd Bialer. Neurophysicist."

"Neuro what?"

The mirror went silent for a second.

"No idea. But that's written on the file our agent sent."

Although contacts between the Living and the Dead were strictly forbidden, the Boss had special access to the other world. Black ops no one knew about except for Joe M. and a few others. The Boss had explained to him that these contacts were necessary to prevent trouble, but he hadn't explained what kind of trouble he meant. Well, *this* kind of trouble, obviously.

Joe M. looked at the Boss, or rather at his own reflection in the smoking mirror. The detective seemed longer and thinner than he had imagined. Then he became shorter and fatter. Never trust images.

"So what should I do?"

The mirror seemed to think, if a mirror could seem to think.

"The Karma fabric is thinning," the Boss said. "Very annoying. I would even say, if I were pessimistic, critical."

Joe M. waited, knowing the Boss was thinking aloud. It could take a while.

"However, there are ways. Not necessarily karmic ways, but ways nonetheless. We have to contact that Bailer guy. He is the only hope we have."

"That's pretty pessimistic, Boss," Joe M. said, slightly ironically.

"No, Joe. It's optimistic. We could have no hope at all."

Joe nodded, wondering if the Boss could see him. He never mentioned anything about his appearance, clothes, attitude. Joe even wondered if he would notice if he smoked a cigarette. Following this thought, his hand reached for his package.

"Bailer is the weakest link in the situation," the Boss continued. "His empathic readings are very high. We have to find a way to contact him."

Joe M. lit his cigarette.

"I thought it was forbidden to contact anyone," the detective remarked. "We arrested that couple a few months back precisely because of that. And they've been condemned to Random Reincarnation, which is a pretty severe sentence."

"I know, I know," replied the Boss, irritated. "But sometimes laws must be broken in order to protect the higher laws. And you might have found the solution."

"Me?"

Smoke stung Joe's eyes, making him wince. No reaction from the Boss. He was blind as a bat. Suddenly the office door opened and one of the Winged Monkeys came in. Without a word, he snatched Joe's cigarette and walked out, slamming the door behind him.

Joe felt a chill run down his spine. *What the hell?*

"Yes. Go back to your business and let me think. I'll contact you."

Joe M. nodded and left. On the way out, he stared hard at the Winged Monkey standing guard in front of the door. He was almost sure he could smell tobacco on its breath.

5. PISS YELLOW

1. CASTLES IN THE CLOUDS

1.

WARREN WAS ECSTATIC. He had been looking at the live footage of the visit to the Land of the Dead—"Thanatia," as they would call it for advertising and marketing purposes—and had been more than pleased with what he had seen. Hell, he wanted a house like that too! He rose as Spector walked into his office. She was alone, as requested. Security and confidentiality reasons. Of course. He grabbed both her ice-cold hands.

"Please, sit down, sit down . . . "

They sat across the desk from each other, the old man in his worn out leather arm-chair—his "throne" as he liked to call it—and the world-famous architect on the uncomfortable Danish design chair.

"Great work! Really terrific! I am in awe!"

Spector looked at the old man and flashed a razor-thin smile.

"Of course," she said.

"Yes, yes . . . I knew you were perfect for the job . . . When can we take pictures and advertise it?"

Spector frowned

"Pictures?"

"Yes—pictures. I need pictures for the website and the leaflets. Otherwise nobody is going to believe us."

"Professor Bailer told us we couldn't take pictures. Something to do with the shifting of worlds . . . planes . . . realities . . . whatever. We tried to photograph the images on screen, but nothing appears. Weird."

Warren frowned.

"Yes, yes," he said while nodding again.. "I remember now. Too bad, really. We'll have to think of something else. Cannot sell a billion dollar house without a picture, right? Or a virtual tour?"

Spector nodded.

"We can always use computer-generated images," Spector said. "Some of them look even more real than reality itself. I have all the blueprints of the house. Easy to construct a virtual 3-D model. Then we put it in a reconstructed Thanatia, and we say it's the real McCoy . . . And organize a visit for those who are really interested."

"Genius!" Warren cried. "Of course! Oh, how I love machines!"

Spector felt like objecting; although computers were indeed machines, it was more a question of programming, but then again, what was the point?

"When can it be ready, do you think?"

Spector shrugged.

"I'm an architect, not a programmer. I'll ask my studio, if you want."

"Yes, yes, do that! And when you're done, we can go public! Wonderful!"

Spector nodded briefly, and Warren walked her to the door. He took her ice-cold hands in his once more and smiled as she tried to free herself from his skeleton-puppet grip.

As the elevator doors closed behind her, she hoped Thanatia was so huge she would never meet him up there. To spend an eternity with George Warren would be the best proof that Hell did, indeed, exist.

2.

Warren carefully closed the door to his office and winked at Rose, his secretary for the last thirty-five years. He thought he should fire her before she reached the fateful thirty-seven, where he would be obliged to pay all her benefits. He hated to think like that, but then again, life was hard. Nobody knew how much it broke his heart every time he had to get rid of a good employee. Edie had consoled him many times, as he cried on her large, soft breasts. "So sensitive," Edie used to say."My little baby, oh my poor little baby." Warren felt tears rush to his eyes and took out a handkerchief to blow his nose.

No need to think about that now, he told himself, we have something to celebrate.

The Thanatia project was going along great, even better than expected. It was a thrilling business venture—the most thrilling ever, he felt. It made him identify with the bankers who had loaned money to Christopher Columbus. Same courage, same audacity, same craziness.

He smiled as he sat back in his favorite armchair.

Crazy, crazy old man, I am, he thought with a smile. *But crazy old man with a plan . . .*

He reached into the inner pocket of his jacket and pulled out a delicately cream-colored envelope. His name has been inscribed in beautiful black italics, as well as his office address. There was no sender name. Same procedure every year. Warren chuckled softly. He opened the envelope, but didn't take out the letter. He had already read it and knew it by heart. Same invitation every year. One of the few routines he enjoyed, with the annual blow-job in the Jacuzzi of his summer house. Ah, dear, dear Edie . . . His thoughts almost veered for a moment, but he focused back on the letter. The Binderberg Club's annual reunion, the yearly meeting of the 100 richest and most powerful people on the planet . . . What a perfect place for some good funeral Tupperware party-launching! All those power-mongers would *love* Thanatia. They would accept his business card and call him later. Yes, the Binderberg Club—so secret, expensive, perfect. This time, he would bring Edie and that mad scientist of his; they would be impressed and they would impress, Edie with her sweet naïve beauty, and Bailer with his pure honest genius. Edie would distract and lure, Bailer would convince and sell. both unknowingly. Warren couldn't help but feel proud of himself and his grandiose schemes. He bent down to turn on the built-in desk stereo. A few seconds later, a French Foreign Legion version of *La Marseillaise* made the walls of his office tremble. He stood up, putting his little hand on his bulging stomach and began to sing along, almost howling with glee, "*Allons enfants de la patri-i-e . . .*"

2. BAD KARMA, GOOD KARMA

1.

THE PRANKSTER CRIMINALS Jeffrey Ruben and Nancy Custer were sitting on the other side of a barren steel table in the Karma Detention Center's visiting room, looking good in spite of the white prisoner overalls they both wore. A winged monkey guard sat on another chair across the room, doing crosswords in the daily paper.

The winged monkey who had escorted Joe M. through the numerous gates and corridors let him walk alone into the room, and locked the door behind him.

"So Moriarty, we meet again," Nancy greeted the P.I, with a sarcastic smile.

"Shouldn't I be the one saying that?" Joe M. asked, taking a seat in front of them.

Nancy shrugged and looked away, as if she was already bored.

"I'm here to cut a deal with you," Joe said.

It was Jeffrey's turn to sneer.

"The Old Man must be really desperate."

Joe M. flashed a tight smile.

"Well, actually, yes, he is. We are facing a . . . situation . . . and we need your help."

Nancy looked back at him, and Joe could see she was trying to evaluate his words.

"Our help? What's in it for us?"

"Immediate pardon. All your files erased. Free to go. Completely."

"Files? What files?" Nancy asked, playing dumb.

Joe M. sighed.

"Listen, I'm not here to talk politics. I'm just the messenger here, trying to help everybody. Don't shoot me."

"What situation?" Jeffrey asked, back on track.

"The Karmic Balance. It's being threatened. Seriously."

"By another group of your so-called 'terrorists'?" Nancy snapped. "We have no connections with anybody else, and if we did, we wouldn't tell you."

"That's right," Jeffrey agreed.

Joe M. shook his head.

"Not terrorists, this time. Real estate sharks."

Nancy frowned.

"I don't get this."

Joe M. wobbled his head.

"It's very complicated. That's why the Old Man, as you call him, is ready to cancel the Reincarnation sentence in exchange for your help."

"I still don't get this," Nancy muttered.

"Wait a minute," Jeffrey said, suddenly lighting up. "Those real estate sharks—where do they come from?"

"Exactly," Joe M. said. "My car is outside. The Old Man is waiting for us."

2.

"Thanks," Nancy said, accepting Joe M's cigarette.

She was sitting next to him in the green Dodge Dart, with Jeffrey and a winged monkey in the backseat. Joe wondered if the monkey smoked. He offered him one, which the beast accepted. Jeffrey took one too. The grey cloud that soon rose gave them all a feeling of togetherness as they drove towards the Boss's villa. Still, seeing the winged monkey smoke was really weird.

3.

The three of them sat down in front of the large smoking mirror. Two winged monkeys guarded the door and a third came in, pushing a small cart propped with expensive liquor.

"All power to the people," Jeffrey said, pouring himself a half-glass of vodka on the rocks, with a thin slice of lime.

"By any means necessary," Nancy added, grabbing the bottle of bourbon.

Joe said nothing, but raised the cognac bottle.

The smoke changed color, shifting from a deep red to a blinding gold. Joe knew the Boss was about to speak.

"Welcome to you all," the voice said, louder than necessary. "Thank you for agreeing to come here. As you know, the situation is critical. Joe must have told you."

Nancy nodded, then turned to Joe and whispered in his ear, "Can he see us?"

Joe was tempted to tell her that he could see everything, but it was a lie and he didn't like propaganda, so he just shrugged.

"What do you mean, 'critical'?" Jeffrey asked. "You know the Karmic Balance is a lie, created to oppress the non-living!"

"I wish you were right," the mirror sighed, sounding almost human for a second. Joe wondered if his theory about a little man sitting behind the mirror surrounded by ultra-advanced machinery was correct after all.

"Unfortunately, it is a scientific fact. To cut a long story short, let's say that it is the fabric sometimes called the "Dark Matter" that keeps our universe together. "

"Man, you sound like you smoked too much in your youth," Nancy said, putting down her glass.

The mirror ignored her remark.

"And you look like it too," she added.

"*All* of the universe—that means all of its different layers, of which we are a part . . . The fabric must be kept intact in order for this universe to exist. If the fabric is ripped, the whole thing goes to hell. Not literally, of course, but you get the picture. We will be wiped out. Completely wiped out. And right now, the Living are destroying this fabric. Fast. They have created a rip that keeps getting larger and larger, like a stocking with a run in it."

"Not good," Jeffrey said. "We want a revolution, not an explosion."

"Not *that kind* of explosion at least," Nancy added.

"You see," the mirror added, after a pause (for effect? Joe

wondered.) "When you make these prank phone calls, you add to the instability. If ten of you did the same thing, we would be in serious trouble . . . "

"We are legion," Jeffrey said, lifting his fist.

"Now imagine, that what the living are doing is the equivalent of a thousand of you . . . "

"We are legion," Nancy said in her turn, her voice slightly less assured than her companion's and without raising her fist.

Joe M. felt like telling them to shut up, but he thought the Boss might resent this. Paternalism was the Boss's thing and he surely didn't want to lose his prerogative.

"So you want us to stop them," Nancy said again, shaking a loose blonde hair from her face. "How?"

"Yeah, how?" Jeffrey said. "Seriously."

"I have an idea," the mirror said, slightly changing color. "It's a long shot, but it might work."

Nancy and Jeffrey turned to Joe M., but the detective shrugged. The Boss hadn't told him his plan.

"And that's why you're here," the mirror resumed. "You need to make a phone call."

3. DEAD TONE

1.

WHEN TODD BAILER came home, Violet was in front of the TV, watching the news. He felt both proud and uneasy as he hung his jacket in the small lobby of their house. It was the first time he would really lie to her. It was the first time he had a secret that weighed so heavily on his shoulders.

"There is something wrong with the answering machine," Violet yelled as the scientist filled himself a glass of water in the kitchen. "There are five messages, but you can only hear static."

Bailer's throat ached and he gulped down the water before walking into the sitting room.

"Hi," he said, trying to sound as normal as possible. "Had a good day? I'll check the machine. You expecting a call?"

Violet shook her head.

"No, but I just think it's annoying. I hate it when technology fails. Especially since I hate technology."

There were 5 messages on the machine, or so the numeral said. Bailer pushed the button and listened. Electric winds. Howling hail. Gravel tornado. Violet was right. There was a problem. He was about to erase them when the phone rang, startling him.

"Allô?"

"Professor Bail . . . Baileor . . . must come . . . "

The voice was very weak.

"Come where?"

There was a pause, filled in by the noise of a thousand electronic crickets. It seemed to him that he could hear a couple more voices, however, speaking to each other.

"Where?" he repeated, about to put the receiver down.

"A . . . Abydos . . . "

"Abdi-what?"

"Abydos . . . "

There was a strange sound, then the line was dead.

"Who was that?" Violet asked, still sitting on the sofa.

"No idea," Todd said, joining her. "Maybe a prank call."

"One of your disgruntled employees?"

"Nobody got fired in my department."

Violet shrugged, as if she knew better. But he knew it wasn't anybody from the lab. They had actually hired two technicians last month, and he hadn't recognized the voice. Probably a random prank. Still, he thought, he would check out that name. After dinner. After he told her the lie he was supposed to tell her.

Warren had been very clear about that: "This is top secret. Your life depends on it. Your wife can't know what I am about to tell you."

Sitting alone in front of Warren in his private office was scary enough for Bailer. But this, on top of it all . . .

"Even Spector won't know about this. Nobody but you, me and Edie. And the bodyguards, of course. Can't do without them."

Warren had leaned back in his armchair, grunting as he furrowed his brow.

"This is of the utmost importance, Bailer. It's part of a huge secret marketing plan I have devised for Thanatia. It will be officially unveiled at the Binderberg Club reunion next weekend, and you're going to present it."

Bailer saw Violet's face float right before his eyes, pale with rage. She would kill him. She would strangle him with his tie and set fire to his pants. The Binderberg! The secret club at the heart of every conspiracy theory . . . Probably the most hated collection of power-mongers in the world—and he would be part of it. Impossible. Ridiculous. Pathetic.

"But . . . but . . . I can't," Bailer had stuttered, in shock.

Warren had snorted, like a wild pig.

"You will, Bailer. And Edie will be coming too. You'll see, she's a beautiful woman. Not that you should care. But she is."

"A penny for your thoughts," Violet said suddenly.

Bailer snapped out of his painful reverie.

"Uh, I was thinking that I'm hungry . . . What's for dinner?" he asked.

"I'm tired," Violet said. "Let's order some pizza."

Bailer nodded. Pizza was always good. Heavy enough to get one ready to tell a big lie.

2.

"Abydos: city in ancient Egypt, also nicknamed the City of the Dead."

Bailer scratched his head as he stared at his laptop's screen. This didn't make any sense. Some kind of stupid prank, as he had thought at first. Or a threat? He smirked, and shrugged. Who would want to threaten him? The project he worked on was completely secret, and the last time he had failed a student was eons ago, when he was still teaching at the university. He couldn't imagine an old student suddenly waking up with a grudge.

Violet had gone to bed right after dinner. She had a long day at school tomorrow, with some of her most difficult classes. He decided to join her and read too. He was half-way through a great thriller. Perfect after that phone call.

3.

"To New Babylon? Next weekend? What are you going to do there?"

"It's a work meeting, with some investors."

Bailer was glad they had turned off the lights. He had never been a good liar.

"And they want you to come along?"

"Yes, I have to describe the technicalities of the project. Give it some scientific credit."

"I thought you were considered a loony . . . "

Bailer knew that Violet wasn't saying this to be mean, but because it was true. His name was present on all the webpages dedicated to afterlife experiences and whatnot. He had stopped searching for his name on the web. Too depressing.

"Not by everybody. I did get a job with the Warren Corporation, didn't I?"

"Yes, and I still don't know what you're doing there. You're a neurophysicist."

Bailer sighed.

"I told you they want to expand. I'm part of a confidential project. I can't tell you what it is before it is made public . . . I'm sorry:"

Violet grunted and turned her back to him. *If it is ever made public,* he should have said. Who knew what Warren had in mind?

Bailer thought about the Land of the Dead and that beautiful city that expanded for miles and miles. What would happen to it? Would Warren build his Necropolis on the beautiful beaches only, or would he want more? Would they eventually spread salt all over the city and lay it in ruins, so they could build more? He wanted to think "no, of course not," but his heart said "Yes, of course they will." A weight landed on his chest, as if someone had dropped an anvil made of shadow. He had always thought that bad conscience weighed on the shoulders. Now he knew otherwise.

4.

"Todd, wake up . . . The phone . . . "

Merging from a cloud of blackness, Bailer sat up in the bed, trying to collect his thoughts. The phone. Yes. Ringing.

He got up and felt his way down the stairs. He managed to get to the phone without walking into a wall or banging a toe against anything, which amazed him.

Still half-sleeping, he lifted the receiver up.

"Yes?"

"You . . . must . . . help . . . us . . . "

"Is this a joke? Help who?"

The voice seemed to come from very far away, almost a whisper.

"You . . . must . . . come . . . to . . . Abydos . . . very . . . soon . . . "

"Not funny. Not funny at all. I'm not going to Egypt because of a prank."

There was a silence filled with electric echoes.

"Not Egypt . . . Land of the dead . . . "

The conversation was abruptly cut, as if a velvety guillotine blade had ruptured a wire. Then the familiar long tone of the dead line.

Bailer frowned. Dead line. Land of the Dead. Spooky voice.

Walking back up the stairs, he suddenly felt a chill down his spine.

Not a prank.
Definitely not a prank.
Then what?
"Who was that?" Violet mumbled, half-asleep.
"There is a problem at the lab," he lied, looking for his clothes. "An emergency."
"Serious?"
"I don't know yet."
No, not a prank.

5.

What was he doing here? Bailer looked around the empty lab and shivered, but it wasn't from the cold. Sneaking in in the middle of the night was somewhat eerie. He stared at one of the video cameras tracking his movements as he walked towards a stretcher. How was he going to explain this if anyone asked? That he needed a death fix? A heavenly overdose? Frowning, he sat on the stretcher and picked up a small vial. He remembered the first time, with He-Who-Has-Six-Eyes. So much had happened since then. Shaking his head, he unscrewed the vial's top, lifted it to his lips and gulped down its contents.

4. NOTHING SHORT OF TOTAL WAR

1.

TWO THOUSAND DOLLARS?? Do I hear two thousand dollars??"

Edie nodded and Warren winced inside. Two thousand dollars for an ugly ashtray, a complete waste of money. Neither of them even smoked.

"Two thousand dollars for this vintage 1960 Parisian ashtray given by the First Lady from her own collection. Do I hear Twenty-one hundred?"

Edie nodded again.

"Twenty-two hundred!"

A used ashtray, on top of that. Edie turned her beautiful face towards him, and smiled. He smiled back and patted her hand. The chair was killing him. Couldn't they at least use comfortable chairs for their stupid event? All the people around them were at least millionaires, and some, like him, even billionaires. What a lack of respect . . . Maybe even voluntary. Charities. Fuck charities. The poor and needy wouldn't even get all the money these bastards raised. After paying all the members of the charity board, their assistants and their assistants' assistants, there would only be peanuts left. But everybody would have a good conscience and sleep happy. And that was the point, wasn't it? The Catholic Church had invented indulgences, capitalist charities. Passport to Heaven. Massacre the infidels and their children, pollute the waters, exploit the needy and buy yourself a good night's sleep.

"Twenty-four hundred!"

One thing Warren wasn't was a hypocrite, and he was mighty proud of that. If he had lived in the Wild West, he wouldn't have said "Sorry" to the Injuns. He would've said, "Fuck you and the horse I killed you on." And he wouldn't have gone to church either, singing hymns and patting little children on the head. No— the world was a battlefield and he was one of the ruthless warlords. Each and every skyscraper he had built, each and every parcel house he had constructed was a flag of victory on the global map. And soon, on the cosmic map.

"Sold for $Twenty-six hundred to Mrs. Edie Warren! A round of applause, guys!"

Edie stood up, clapping and screaming like a little girl.

2.

Warren gave the evil eye to the $2600 ashtray now decorating the desk in his office. He felt like Dracula if his wife had bought him a crucifix. "Here, darling! I thought it would look so nice on your vintage ebony desk!" Such a sweet, sweet person, Edie. Sometimes he could puke. He sighed and closed the file he was looking at. Another project in some fuckaway desert. Yeah, as if he had any time to waste . Earthly projects bored him to death—literally. He had the ultimate project of all time—Thanatia! Sometimes he couldn't believe his luck. As some poet had written once: "I believe in Karma/The bad guys always get/all the good stuff." Absolutely. Good, evil, all of that was bullshit. Survival of the richest was the only thing that mattered. Morals were for sissies. Finding out about the Land of the Dead hadn't changed his perspective a bit. They hadn't seen any angels, right? Or any demons, for that matter. The reports had spoken of "pale shadows," like very old photographs. Fuck shadows. Who needed shadows? They also spoke of some city in the distance, at least, that's what Bailer had said. He claimed he had even visited it, but then again, Warren didn't quite buy that. All mad scientists are mad, right? And, even if he was, in his own way, a genius, Bailer was indeed a mad scientist. Hell, you just had to surf a bit on the internet, and there it was—"Mad death guru," "The Man Who Discovered Heaven," and what not.

Warren had been more than skeptical in the beginning. But his sixth sense had been right: there was money to be made out of this. Tons of money. And maybe more. Warrenland. Why not?

Warren opened an envelope and unfolded a large piece of paper. His own manor in Thanathia. Beautiful, Frank Lloyd Wright-style, with the best view on the ocean. The first sale would pay for its construction. Now the question was— what about Edie? Would he build a room for her? The girl sure deserved it, but then again, she would be his widow and then, who knows? Another man, some charming gigolo . . . No way would he accept an unfaithful woman in his house for eternity . . . With her gigolo on top of that . . . Maybe he would build a guest room that could be transformed later . . . Or a guest pavilion, in the garden. Even better. Yes, that was a good idea. He would speak to Spector about that.

He shrugged and folded the plan back into the envelope. Death was making him think too much. Fuck death.

5. MEANWHILE, BACK AT THE CELESTIAL RANCH

1.

TODD, WONDERFUL TO see you! We were all hoping you would come."

Joe M. welcomed him on the wind-beaten beach with a warm smile. Bailer couldn't remember feeling any breeze the last time he had come, during the visit to the construction site. Joe M.'s hair flew around his face like a dark furry halo.

"My pleasure," Bailer answered, not really knowing what to say. "Sure is windy today."

Joe M. nodded.

"The Boss says it's a consequence of the Karma ripping. That, and the disease."

Bailer was at a loss.

"I'm sorry, but I don't know what you're talking about . . . ."

Joe M. had a little dry laugh.

"No, no, of course you don't. The Boss will explain."

Joe M. began to walk back towards his car, which was parked on the side of the road, a few hundred yards away. Bailer felt the sand give way under his weight. Somehow, it felt like a perfect symbol of the whole situation, and he carefully watched his steps not to trip and fall,

2.

Sitting next to the detective, Bailer could admire the landscape leading to the city. It felt eerily familiar, the soft green hills rolling

84

on the left-hand side, the deep blue ocean crashing on the yellow beach and black rocks on the right, and the grey road unfolding before them like a concrete carpet. He could see the city of the Dead in the distance, an impossibly huge array of squares, domes and triangles, shining under the cloudless azure sky like a mad Lego construction.

The engine of the Dodge Dart ran smoothly, growling like a happy tiger. Bailer felt nervous. No one is summoned to the land of the Dead without seriously wondering what it's all about. The scientist feared it had to do with the Thanatia situation and dreaded he would be met by Anubis, Horus and all the traditional judges of the Land of the Dead, holding a scale to weigh his sins. The voice had called him to Abydos, hadn't it?

"I didn't know the city was called Abydos," Bailer said faintly.

Joe M. shot him a sideways glance and smiled.

"It isn't. In fact, it has no name. But it was Jeffrey's idea, to convince you it wasn't just a prank call. He said you would check the name out and understand. Apparently, he was right, too."

"Jeffrey?"

"Too long to explain, but you will meet him. You guys will work together. And with Nancy too. We just have to figure the whole thing out."

Bailer nodded, feeling powerless. Maybe he had overdosed. Maybe all of this was a just a surreal construction of his guilt-ridden mind.

"We're here," Joe M. said, slowing down and stopping before a huge, gold painted, iron-wrought portal guarded by two winged monkeys in red uniforms. The portal opened and the monkeys gave a military salute as they drove past.

That was it: the final OD.

3.

The mansion was incredible—huge, high and yellow. A mix of Gothic English and Spanish Baroque, it looked like a crazy 30s millionaire's Bel-Air villa, like the ones Bailer had sometimes seen in documentaries on Hollywood's golden age.

The detective parked the car in front of the house, at the bottom of the large, yellow marble steps.

"You may not know this," Joe M. said, "but you're the first Living person to come here, ever. And hopefully, the last," he added with a smirk.

Bailer, his thoughts swirling like frightened birds inside his skull, followed the detective up the marble steps, wondering if he would ever leave this place again. Alive, he meant. But then again, that was self-explanatory.

4.

Joe M. rang the bell and the large wooden double-doors opened, revealing yet another uniformed winged monkey who let them in. The creature wobbled before them, leading them through a maze of long corridors and strangely furnished rooms. There were all sorts of styles and periods mashed together, as if the owner wanted to confuse the visitors and did a fantastic job at it.

"I hate those monkeys," the detective whispered in Bailer's ear as they trod through yet another room. "They give me the creeps."

The professor nodded. He was glad he wasn't the only one.

They finally arrived at the end of a long corridor, barred by a small grey-painted normal-looking door. Bailer thought it looked like those doors you see in hospitals. The monkey knocked three times, loudly, then opened the door without waiting for an answer. Bailer's mouth gaped in awe. The room was enormous, with walls covered with what looked like huge precious stones. A massive Baroque crystal chandelier hung from the ceiling, making the stones glitter and shedding an incredibly soft and soothing light all around. There was a tapestry representing the villa itself covering the furthest wall, but the scene was woven in a mixture of different styles: Egyptian, Sumerian, medieval and Persian, among those he could recognize.

There were four leather armchairs arranged around a small round table. The monkey pulled a chair out and waved to Bailer, who sat down. Joe M. took the one next to him.

"Jeffrey and Nancy will be joining us shortly," the detective told him.

As if on cue, the small door opened again and a couple walked in, escorted by another monkey. The man was in his late twenties, wearing a cream-colored suit over a white t-shirt. He had shoulder-length brown hair and a wild beard. His eyes were almost black, and burned with a strange fire. The woman seemed younger, a beautiful blonde in a 60s multicolored dress, with deep blue eyes and an ironic smirk pasted on her lips. Both were barefoot.

"Jeffrey Ruben. Nancy Custer. Professor Todd Bailer. You all know who I am," Joe M. said as they rose, shook hands with the couple and sat down again.

The tapestry suddenly began to rise and a huge oval mirror appeared, covering the entire wall and filled with psychedelic colored smoke. Bailer thought it looked somewhat cheap, but kept his big mouth shut.

"We're all here, Boss," Joe M. said to the mirror, which changed color to a deep pulsating red.

Cool, Bailer thought.

"Ladies and gentlemen," the mirror said in a strange high-pitched voice, "welcome. You all know why we are here, except for Mr. Bailer, to whom we owe an explanation."

Fifteen minutes later, Bailer looked at each of the others in turn, then back at the mirror.

"Shit," he said.

5.

"Let me see if I got everything right," Bailer resumed. "If the living manage to invade the Land of the Dead, as they seem to be planning to do, the whole karmic balance will rip, the Universe with it and no one knows what will happen next, but it will surely not be good . . . "

Joe M., Jeffrey and Nancy nodded slowly.

"Exactly," the mirror said. "That's why we need your help."

Bailer added confusion to his panic.

"But how?"

"We have to stop this Warren and his project," the mirror said. "Maybe you could kill him."

"Whoa, bad karma, dude!" Jeffrey protested.

"Could look like an accident," the mirror offered.

"Karma is karma," Nancy said. "You know you can't cheat karma. This poor man here will be immediately reincarnated when he dies without any trial, and I think it's not fair."

"He did help on the Thanatia project," the mirror said.

"He couldn't know what the consequences were," Joe M. said. "For once I agree with Jeff and Nancy, Boss. I'm sorry."

"But what's a little reincarnation compared to the whole karmic balance going to hell?" the mirror pleaded.

Everybody became silent.

"I can't kill anybody," Bailer said. "I have never used a gun and I faint at the sight of my own blood."

"We have to find a solution," the mirror resumed. "The situation is critical."

"Maybe a phone call could scare him," Jeffrey offered. "They work pretty well."

"Or we could make a phone call and send a poltergeist through the lines," Nancy added. "That works really well too."

Bailer saw Joe M.'s eyebrow slightly rise at the suggestions.

"What have you been up to that I don't know about, you two . . . ?" he asked the couple.

"Enough, Joe," the mirror said. "They've got full pardon for their past misdemeanors. You know that."

"Sure, Boss. Whatever you say. But poltergeists are way out of line . . . "

"And I don't think it would work," Bailer said. "Ghosts cannot stop anything, as far as I know. They can smash things, make eerie noises and glow in the dark, but they never say anything that makes sense. Warren is a logical man, he wouldn't get it. Would probably think he ate something bad the previous night. "

"Maybe if we got him alone here and explained the whole thing to him," Nancy said. "Hey, that's a swell idea! That could work!"

The mirror changed color to a deep green.

"We are already pushing the karmic limit with Professor Bailer here. I can feel it. I'm afraid the disease might reach new heights after his departure."

"Disease?" Bailer asked. "In the Land of the Dead?"

The mirror sighed.

"I know, I know. Sounds impossible, but since the construction of that house on the beach, people here seem to have been contaminated by some strange case of sexual rabies—an irresistible need to make love right here, right now. Never happened before—

we don't need to make love here. Death is decent. Death is safe. Death is respectful. But recently . . . "

"Bad craziness all around," Nancy said, shaking her head.

"Crazy shit," Jeffrey confirmed.

"We have quarantined the sick, but don't know what to do with them. Shall we wait until they get cured, if that is possible? Shall we reincarnate them? But how can you condemn someone to reincarnation when they're not really guilty?" the mirror said. "Oh my, oh my, oh my . . . "

"Things really *do* sound bad," Bailer said, his mind suddenly drifting to Violet. What would she think? What would she do? She always said that laughter was the best weapon. Yes, laughter . . .

"Maybe we can pull a prank," Bailer resumed. "Make Warren look so bad or ridiculous nobody would want to touch him, or his project."

"Great idea!" the mirror said, turning golden. "But how?"

There was a long moment of silence. Jeff whispered something into Nancy's ear, but she shook her head. Joe M. scratched his head. Bailer suddenly jumped to his feet.

"The Electric Cool-Aid Acid Test!"

Joe M., Nancy and Jeff looked up at him, obviously not getting it. The mirror's smoke turned grey.

"What?" Joe M. said.

"The Electric Kool-Aid Acid Test!" Bailer said again, his voice now high-pitched. "In the Sixties, this band, the Grateful Dead, they laced free Kool-Aid with LSD, making people trip during their show . . . We could do the same thing to Warren—turn the whole thing into some crazy circus . . . The media would be there, of course . . . Waiting outside . . . "

"What the hell are you talking about, dude?" Jeffrey finally asked.

"What thing? What circus?" the mirror asked.

Bailer was trembling with excitement.

"I've got this invitation, for this weekend . . . To the Bindenberg Club . . . I could pour some stuff in his glass and make him trip in public . . . He would completely make a fool of himself, and nobody would have anything to do with him anymore . . . "

Joe M. looked at the mirror. It was a pulsating deep blue, ebbing on purple.

"What do you think, Boss? Sounds like we might have a plan."
The mirror hummed.

"How would you get the drug into Warren's glass? Everybody would see you . . . Him first, probably. And the place will be packed with security, no doubt."

Bailer sat down, frowning.

"Yes, you're right. I don't know. I hadn't thought about that."

"Maybe you could bribe one of the waiters," Joe M. said, but it was obvious he didn't believe in his own idea.

"You could use a special ring, like the Borgias," Jeff suggested, not seeming much convinced either.

Nancy raised her hand, like a beautiful schoolgirl. They all looked at her, waiting.

"How about . . . a ghost?" she said, smiling.

6. OMEGA GRAY

1. "LET'S SYNCHRONIZE WATCHES"

1.

THE HOUSE WAS almost finished. Actually, it wasn't a house. It was a mansion. It was terrifyingly huge. The whole zone had been declared off-limits, and a detachment of cops surveyed it day and night. The contaminated zone had spread enormously, marked with its eerie salt lines. Joe M. passed the binoculars to Daisy. He had taken her along because she wanted to see for herself.

"Wow!" she said. "This is enormous!"

She put down the binoculars and stared at the detective.

"I'm scared, Joe. What's going to happen to us? I mean, to all of us here."

The detective shrugged, slightly disappointed she hadn't meant "them," as "he" and "she."

"I've no idea, Daisy. I just hope our plan will work out."

Daisy brought the binoculars up to her eyes again. The hard wind moved her jet black hair in dark waves and Joe could see that she had goose bumps on her arms in spite of the shining bright sun.

Something moved and cracked in him.

He hoped he wasn't being infected by the disease.

2.

Warren was very excited. His new *Thanatia* visit cards had arrived from the printers. He was holding one in his hand. It shone, all white and gold, lit up by the sun cutting obliquely through the large window of his office. The Bindenberg Club would be a blast—his best business scheme in half a century, after the New Paris 30th arrondissement contract. What a coup de maître! Nobody would see it coming—the new frontier beyond the new frontier, literally. What's more, he would be able to enjoy his success in the afterlife, forever. He suddenly remembered he had to add something important in his will.

Like an old Chinese emperor, he would require to be buried with his collection of army figures.

3.

Todd Bailer had never felt so nervous. He was filling up his suitcase for his weekend "escapade" and his hands were actually trembling as he placed his ties over his shirts. If being invited to the Binderberg Club was already stressful in itself, being an accessory to the drugging of George Warren made him sweat non-stop. Violet was at work and he wouldn't see her before he caught his plane. A limo dispatched by Warren would be waiting in front of their building in exactly forty minutes. Time was money, money was time—and both sucked. Bailer wondered if he should write a goodbye note to his wife, but decided against it. He was only going for a weekend after all. He was also blatantly lying to her, and he knew that she hated dishonesty above all. To her, all power structures, corporations and political parties were "dishonest." And here he was now. She had been right on one point: power and money did corrupt the soul. He was the living proof of that, albeit a naïve one. He suddenly wondered if Werner von Braun had been a naïve soul too: "Wouldn't it be *wunderbar* if we could fly a rocket to the moon?" And blam! goes London. And blam! goes Coventry. He zipped his suitcase closed. It looked like a coffin.

2. COUNTDOWN

1.

WARREN WAS PLEASED they had given him the same room as last year in the Bindenberg Club residence. He loved the view of the lake, and the Old England style furniture. Edie was unpacking their luggage and he felt like a good cigar. He opened the double doors to the balcony and took a cigar out of his coat. It was early spring and still chilly, although the sun was shining over the surrounding woods, reflecting in the lake's dark blue waters. The residence was strictly non-smoking, but he didn't give a damn. Together, the members of the Club owned the fucking country. THEY made the laws, THEY decided what was good and what was bad, THEY owned the media and pretended to defend democracy. Warren chuckled, lighting his cigar. Fuck the innocent, fuck the imbeciles, fuck the fucking lot of them.

2.

Joe M. was sitting in the Boss's main office, tapping nervously on the desk while the mirror showed dark grey smoke. The detective couldn't help wondering how many mirrors there were in the mansion, and how the Boss managed to be in each and every one of them. Or were they all connected by a series of corridors to the same room? The image of a small balding man with huge machinery behind him flickered in his mind again, but faded quickly. There were more important things going on now.

Nancy and Jeff were sitting across the room, staring at the large red phone in front of them. Joe knew everybody was nervous. And this was really a first in the Land of the Dead.

3.

Todd Bailer looked at the room he had just entered, followed by a porter who put his suitcase down. Bailer didn't know if he should tip the young man or not, but extended him a bill anyway. The stone-faced penguin took it, with a sharp bow of the head. Bailer wondered how much it would cost to get a smile. Beyond his savings, no doubt. The room was pure bad taste luxury, with lots of pastel colors, gilded things and fake art. His eyes caught on the phone, sitting on the little American Revolution desk and he smiled. Joe M. had told him they would leave a line open for him for twenty four hours from his E.T.A. at the hotel, which had been an hour earlier—they had underestimated traffic. All he had to do was press the zero. Joe had explained that the zero on any telephone opened a connection to the Land of the Dead, if you pressed long enough.

Bailer looked at his cheap watch.

He still had a little less than 23hours ahead of him. A good window. He had almost freaked out going through the security checks; metal detectors, glass detectors, sniffing dogs, plastic detectors—the whole shebang. He had fortunately poured the drug he had smuggled from his lab—some extremely powerful hallucinogenic liquid He-Who-Has-Six-Eyes had given him on his last visit—into an small eye-drop vial. Nobody had bothered him about it.

Thinking about what could have happened if he was caught, he felt his knees grow weak. The good news was that, as he had surmised, there would be a cocktail party this evening. It was confirmed in the little schedule he had received upon his check-in. Golden letters on cream paper. Of course. He felt like he was in a James Bond movie. although, if it had been the case, it was unclear whether he would have been the hero or the super-villain.

4.

Edie was tying Warren's bowtie while he looked at himself in the large wardrobe's mirror. An old man helped by a stunning beauty. She wore a golden strapless evening dress, making her look like a 70s glamour queen.

"Don't move," she said.

He could feel her fingers pressing on his throat. She could have strangled him easily. He tried to look into her eyes, but she was entirely focused on the resisting tie. She would be one of the richest widows in the world. He wondered if she ever thought about that, then shrugged. Of course, she did. He sure would.

"Don't move," she repeated.

His hands felt the silver card-holder buried in his pants' pocket. Tonight would be the first step for Thanatia. The house was almost finished now. It only lacked a paint job and furniture. Spector had said all would be ready within four weeks. Edie stuck her tongue out of the corner of her lovely mouth.

"I really hate those ties, you know," she said, smiling.

He chuckled. What a lovely woman. He would be very sorry to die before her and leave her behind. Some days, he regretted the passing of the old tradition of having the wife executed and buried with her royal husband. They could be so happy forever. An idea suddenly shone feebly in his mind, like a gold coin at the bottom of a running stream. He could always have her killed in some "accident" after his death . . . There were people in charge of that . . . He was sure some of his Russian partners knew some of those people. He would discreetly ask them. Maybe this weekend, if he had the chance. It would be absurd to leave such a treasure behind for others to plunder. He smiled at his own thought. He liked it. He liked it a lot. He felt God-like.

"There you go, sweetie," Edie said. "You look like a king."

Warren grunted. Why did she always have to ruin everything?

3. MISSION IMPOSSIBLE

1.

THE PHONE RANG and they all jumped in the air. Joe M. was almost sure he had seen the mirror flicker. Jeffrey shot a quick glance at Nancy.

"You're ready for this?"

She nodded.

"First time I've done this legally. I'm psyched."

Joe M. wondered if the Boss appreciated the irony, but he had given his word: Jeff and Nancy were protected from prosecution during the whole operation. The detective wondered how much this was going to harm the Karmic Balance, and if the Boss really knew what the risks were. Then again, it was better for everybody to think the Boss had things under control.

Nancy picked up the phone.

"Yes, she said. I'm on my way."

2.

Warren entered the ballroom with Edie attached to his left arm. The stares she got from the male guests and the tension he felt in their female counterparts reminded him how beautiful his wife was. *Ah Edie*, he thought, *Edie*. The idea he had earlier flickered in his mind again. A king. The mausoleum. While exchanging nods with various familiar faces, he looked for the one that mattered the most to him at this very moment. Vladimir Sarkov, the Russian CEO of the national gas and oil conglomerate. The one with connections.

They moved to the bar, cutting across tuxedos and beautiful dresses. There he was, filling a glass at the punch bowl. Of course.

Edie's perfume became even more pungent and discreet tears prickled his eyes. *Ah, Edie. You will die like a queen.*

3.

Bailer watched the young woman materialize before his eyes in a cloud of shiny blue spots. It reminded him of the cheap special effects from 80s Sci-Fi movies he liked to watch with Violet once in a while, just for laughs. The thought of his wife actually gave him courage. She would approve of this. He would become the hero of her Revolution. If only he could tell her.

"Hi there," Nancy said.

She floated, transparent, a few feet away from him.

"Can you see me?" she asked.

"Yes, a little, he said. You are standing there."

"And like this?"

She disappeared completely.

"I can't see you anymore," Bailer said. "Where are you?"

He suddenly realized he was speaking to what people usually called a "ghost" and wondered if he was still in a coma, after that plane crash in the jungle.

A vase lifted itself up from the table.

"OK," he said. "Here is the stuff?"

Nancy became slightly visible again and took the eye-drop vial. It literally disappeared in the back pocket of her jeans.

"A shaman I know gave me some very powerful stuff on my last visit. You ready?"

"Of course," she replied, with a devastating smile. "I'm always ready for a little fun."

4.

"How long do we have?" Joe M. asked.

The mirror shimmered and glowed.

"A couple of hours. Our time."

"Can I go out and have a cigarette?" Jeffrey asked.

"I'll go with you," the detective said. "I need a smoke too."

Outside, Joe lit Jeffery's cigarette, then his own.

"You don't seem nervous," the detective said, as Jeff blew smoke through his nostrils.

"Oh, we've done that sort of thing before," the young man said. "Minor scale, of course. But it's the first time we've been part of a Black Ops operation. That is the only thing that would make me slightly nervous."

Joe M. nodded, although he wasn't sure why.

"And I don't believe in that karma shit," Jeff added, looking straight at Joe. "I think it's just a way for the Man to get us to do his dirty work."

The detective shrugged.

"May very well be. But that house is real. Something needs to be done about it. To protect ourselves. You can ask any tribal people here. They would agree immediately."

Jeff nodded.

"I know, I know. I am happy to fuck up that project. But I still don't like working for the Man. We could be doing this on our own. All power to the People, you know."

"Whatever you say," Joe said, taking a long drag.

He really hated these fucking hippies.

5.

Warren was talking to Bill Brett, from Brett Inc., the weapons manufacturer. Edie was at the bar, filling her glass with some exquisite punch. He suddenly noticed Todd Bailer walking in, looking very nervous. Those academics were only good for one thing—their fucking research. Otherwise, they were a complete nuisance. He really hoped that Bailer would be up to the level here. Warren felt for the silver card-holder in his pocket, knowing he was playing with billions and everlasting fame. He waved to Bailer, who walked towards them.

"Bill Brett, Professor Todd Bailer. My latest addition to the corporation."

Bill, a tall balding man with a skull-like face and deeply set black eyes, shook the scientist's hand.

"Nice to meet you. A professor?"

His plastic button eyes veered inquisitively to Warren.

"Are you investing in universities now, Warren? I thought everybody agreed it was a really bad business plan . . . "

"A new project," Warren said. "The Final Frontier. Here, take my card and call me sometime. I'm sure you'll be interested."

Brett took the card that had magically appeared in Warren's hand, nodded a couple of times and excused himself. Warren patted Bailer's shoulder.

"Good," he said, very satisfied. "Very good. Care for a drink? They've got a delicious punch over there . . . "

6.

Bailer was staring at Warren's half-empty glass, wondering if Nancy had already managed to spike his drink.

Warren was holding him by the left elbow, whispering in his ear the names of the famous people chatting around them as they advanced towards the bar. So far, Bailer had only recognized the President and the First Lady.

At the bar, Warren refilled his glass, while Bailer chose a glass of red wine. He didn't want to drink anything too strong. Suddenly, one of the elderly men Warren had just pointed to, a certain Al Greenbottom, from the Greenbottom Bank, fell on all fours and began to bark. A woman next to him laughed hysterically, then proceeded to tear her dress apart, saying "I see you, my God! I see you! I can see you!"

Two plainclothes security officers rushed to them. The first one tried to help Greenbottom to his feet, but his hand got savagely bitten. He let out a chilling howl of pain as his fingers turned red. Meanwhile, the other officer tried to cover up the lady, who kicked him in the balls, screaming, "Satan! Satan! Satan!"

Bailer turned to Warren, completely surprised, but his boss had disappeared. More and more guests were undressing, complaining about the heat. Some were chanting in incomprehensible languages. Others argued, brow against brow, like two deer in a forest stand-off. He saw a beautiful woman sob uncontrollably.

The security people were running from one group to another, trying to calm everybody down. Some of them got kicked or punched.

Bailer felt like everything was happening in slow motion. Nancy appeared before him and winked, before disappearing again. Bailer suddenly understood , and his knees grew weak. She had spiked the punch bowl, not just Warren's glass.

Looking around in panic, he spotted Warren talking to Edie in the corner of the room. She seemed furious with him, spit foaming at the corner of her mouth. He kept repeating, "You're my queen, I'm so sorry, you're my queen . . . " while she yelled, "I hate you and your fucking toys! I hate you, I hate you, I hate you!" Before Bailer could make his way through the unpredictable crowd, he saw Warren seize Edie's throat and squeeze it with all his strength. An officer jumped on him, then another, but to no avail. Edie's face turned blue. Warren was still screaming "You're my queen! My queen! Forever!" Then Edie slumped on the ground and Warren lay on top of her, licking her face like a dog, with the two officers still clutching his shoulders.

EPILOGUE

1.

TODD BAILER WOKE up feeling good. He didn't have to go to work, as he had resigned as executive director of the Thanatia project the day before. After Warren's trial and commitment to a psychiatric ward, they had temporarily asked him to remain in charge of the project. He had sent a team of workers to clear up the salt around the Thanatia mansion, then he fired everybody, erased all the files on the computers and resigned. The Warren Corporation was in so much shit because of the trial and the bad publicity that they hadn't batted an eye and had even given him a bonus for "terminating a financially hazardous project."

When he'd told Violet he had resigned, she smiled and kissed him on the lips.

"What now?" she asked him.

He shrugged.

"Being a New Age guru might not be so bad after all. I think I'm going to write a book or accept one of those TV series offers . . . "

This morning, the TV series idea seemed the best to him. He had been approached by various channels to be the host of some of their "Weird Stories" stuff. At the time, he had laughed them off. Now, he saw the point. To make himself visible on some ridiculous show might help him protect the Land of the Dead, to make people really believe that he was a crackpot theorist. Perfect plan.

Violet was still sleeping. A bright sun shone outside, and Sunday was slowly happening. He thought about what Joe M. had told him, the last time he had visited him after the "Bindenberg Incident", as the media called it. He had finally mustered the courage to ask him about Emily. Where she was. If he could meet her. He had tried to sound casual, matter-of-fact, but his chest had been ripped apart as he had clumsily stammered his questions.

"Do you see any children or babies here?" the detective said, lighting a cigarette.

They were on the beach, near the city, where the Thanatia villa had once stood. The Boss had sent a demolition team a few hours after the last salt was removed. Now only ruins remained, a ghostly reminder. Bailer looked around, glancing at the people strolling on the beach, his heart still slowly burning inside his chest.

"No. No, I don't."

"We don't keep children here. We send them back, directly. In a better place, a good karmic family. We only accept karmic complete people here. Those who had a full life and explored all their allocated potential."

Bailer nodded slowly, letting the info sink in.

"So . . . no Emily?" he finally said.

"No," Joe M. said. "She's someone else now—a happy ten year-old with a bright future."

A happy ten-year old with a bright future. Violet moved slightly and groaned. He kissed her cheek and sat up in bed, longing for some strong coffee. He had never felt so alive.

2.

Joe M. raised his glass and Daisy did the same. The restaurant was crowded. It was a new joint that had just opened in the 70s district, very hip and chic.

"To another solved case," Daisy said.

"Well, I was just an accessory," Joe M. said, modestly. "The Hippies actually did it. And that guy, Bailer."

Daisy smiled. Joe loved the way her nose slightly moved when she smiled.

"Ah, but Joe, you're the one who put the whole team together . . . And I really hope that Warren will be reincarnated as various animals for the next thousand years when he dies . . . "

"Shhhh!" Joe said, leaning over the table so close he could smell her lipstick. "That's his wife, over there. The beautiful blonde . . . "

He lifted his chin in the direction of another table, where a stunningly beautiful young woman was having dinner with a stunningly handsome young man. Daisy nodded, as Joe leaned back.

He felt good. He felt things were back in place. No more strange sexual plague. No more fear of jumping on someone to have public intercourse. Now, only love remained. Pure, quiet, beautiful love. They clinked their glasses together. The crystalline sound remained in his ears long after it had faded. It was the eternal and comforting sound of his soul.

ABOUT THE AUTHOR

Sébastien Doubinsky is a bilingual French writer and academic, born in Paris in 1963. His last two novels, *The Song of Synth* and *White City* were published in the United States, respectively by Talos/Skyhorse and Bizarro Pulp Fiction/JournalStone. He currently lives in Denmark, where he teaches French literature, culture and history at the French department of the University of Aarhus.

Boiled Americans by Matthew Allen Rose

Boiled Americans is a puzzle box in book form, inspired by the violence of living in urban America and exploding the tendency to forget or ignore.

Great American Slasher by David C. Hayes

Baseball, apple pie . . . and murder.

The Bohemian Guide to Monogamy
by Andrew Armacost

Here, a strange labyrinth of interlinked short fiction assembles itself into a darkly moving novella that deftly explores the bottomless pain and pleasure of love and commitment, the hinterland between youth and adulthood.

Surreal Worlds edited by Sean Leonard

An anthology of surrealistic compositions created by some of the finest names in genre fiction. A showcase of international talent undaunted by the conventions of language and common narrative structures. Here is timelessness. Here is Surreal Worlds

How to Succesfully Kidnap Strangers by Max Booth III

Do not respond to bad reviews. If you must respond to bad reviews, please do not kidnap the reviewer.

ADHD Vampire by Matthew Vaughn

He came, he conquered, he was distracted a lot

Notes from the Guts of a Hippo
by Grant Wamack

A rugged journalist travels to Brazil in search of a missing hippo researcher and the notes left behind lead to something earth shatteringly revelatory.

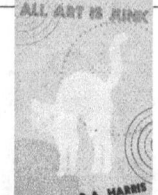

All Art is Junk by R. A. Harris

Lana Rivers, a girl with paintbrush hair, is missing and it's up to Lancelot, her cyborg knight, and his bionic conjoined twin, Cilia, to find her before her evil father, a disrespected artist turned mad-scientist, performs a terrible experiment on her.

Cherub by David C. Hayes

Cherub wasn't like the other boys—too slow, too rough—but he didn't deserve what that hospital did to him, and now he will make them pay.

Skinners by Adam Millard

Los Angeles, the City of Angels. At least, that's what the brochure says. What it fails to mention is the earthquakes. Oh, and the flesh-eating creatures lying dormant beneath the concrete, waiting for the chance to surface once again. Their wait is over . . .

The After-Life Story of Pork Knuckles Malone by MP Johnson

What's a farm boy to do when his pet pig becomes an evil, decaying hunk of ham with slime-spewing psychic powers?

A Lightbulb's Lament by Grant Wamack

A gentleman with a lightbulb for head wakes up in a world full of darkness, hooks up with a beautiful ex-prostitute, and an old man who can heal people; he travels down south to find the mysterious Creator.

The Horror Show by Vincenzo Bilof

A poetry novel—a narcoleptic, amnesiac Nobel Prize-winning poet becomes the subject of an experiment to cure madness.

Beyond by Jordan Krall

From Jerusalem to Mars, psychiatry and the unraveling of the universe

Gravity Comics Massacre
by Vincenzo Bilof

An absolutely shitty novella involving comic books, aliens, a serial killer, teenagers in an abandoned town, horror-trope dream sequences, and an ending you're going to hate.

Glue by Scott Lange

Sticky bowels and sticky situations.

Ascent by Matthew Bialer

Is the 8 foot tall creature haunting a small town in Iowa in the fall of the year 1903 the product of a hoax and collective imagination or was it one of the first documented paranormal event in America? This epic poem grapples with these questions.

Fecal Terror by David Bernstein

A killer turd is on the loose!

The Fairy Princess of Trains
by Christopher Boyle

Danny's mediocre life turns upside-down when his couch starts whispering to him. Then he's charged with a supernatural mission: Rescue the Fairy Princess of Trains.

Terence, Mephisto & Viscera Eyes
by Chris Kelso

9 new science fiction stories from Chris Kelso

Industrial Carpet Drag by Bruce Taylor

Chemicals make you do great things!

Bizarro Bizarro: An Anthology

The finest bizarro short stories from 2013.

Necrosaurus Rex by Nicolas Day

Necrosaurus Rex tells the tale of Martin, a simple janitor, who takes an unfortunate trip through time, becomes a violent mutant, and the father of us all. There's 14 billion years crushed inside these pages, and most of them are pretty nasty.

Day of the Milkman by S. T. Cartledge

In a world dominated by the milk industry, only one milkman survives after a terrible storm sinks all the ships and throws the Great White Sea out of balance.

Moosejaw Frontier by Chris Kelso

An unapologetic disaster of metafiction

The Boy Who Loved Death by Hal Duncan

From blackest humour to bleakest horror, with twisted relish, Hal Duncan's eighteen tales dig into death—and the life that goes with it.